The Joker

Edgar Wallace's amazing career brought him from extreme poverty to fantastic success and wealth. He earned his first pennies as a newspaper-boy, and in turn became ship's cook, milk-roundsman, soldier and reporter in South Africa during the Boer War, special correspondent of the London *Daily Mail*, editor, and writer of best-selling fiction. His output of stories was enormous. His income at one time reached £50,000 a year, yet his open-handed generosity and reckless expenditure often left him short of ready money. He was scriptwriting in Hollywood when he died suddenly in 1932.

THE JOKER

EDGAR WALLACE

Pan Books Ltd London and Sydney

The characters in this book are entirely imaginary
and have no relation to any living person

First published by Hodder & Stoughton Ltd
This edition published 1950 by
Pan Books Ltd, Cavaye Place, London SW10 9PG
ISBN 0 330 02075 7
8th Printing 1975
© Penelope Wallace 1966

Printed in Great Britain by
Hunt Barnard Printing Ltd, Aylesbury, Bucks

1

M R STRATFORD HARLOW was a gentleman with no particular call to hurry. By every standard he was a member of the leisured classes, and to his opportunities for lingering, he added the desire of one who was pertinently curious.

The most commonplace phenomena interested Mr Harlow. He had all the requisite qualities of an observer; his enjoyment was without the handicap of sentimentality, a weakness which is fatal to accurate judgement.

Leonardo da Vinci could stand by the scaffold using the dreadful floor as his desk; and sketch the agonies of malefactors given to the torture. Mr Harlow, no great lover of painters, thought well of Leonardo. He too could stop to look at sights which sent the average man shuddering and hurrying past; he could stop (even when he was really in a hurry) to analyse the colour scheme in an autumn sunset, not to rhapsodise poetically, but to mark down for his own information the quantities of beauty.

He was a large man of forty-eight, fair and slightly bald. His clean-shaven face was unlined, his skin without blemish. Pale blue eyes are not accounted beautiful and the pallor of Mr Harlow's eyes was such that, seeing him for the first time, many sensitive people experienced a shock, thinking he was sightless. His nose was big and long, and of the same width from forehead to tip. He had very red, thick lips that seemed to be pouting even when they were in repose. A rounded chin with a dimple in the centre and unusually small ears, completes the description.

His powerful car was drawn up by the side of the road, its two near wheels on the green verge, and Mr Harlow sat, one hand on the wheel, watching the marshalling of the men in a field. In such moments of contemplative reveries as these, splendid ideas were born in Stratford Harlow's mind, great schemes loomed out of the nowhere which is beyond vision. And, curiously enough, prisons invariably had this inspirational effect.

They were trudging now across the field, led by a lank warder, cheerful, sunburnt men in prison uniform.

Tramp! Tramp! Tramp!

The convicts had reached the hard road and were coming towards him. The leading warder glanced suspiciously at the well-dressed stranger, but the gang were neither abashed nor distressed by this witness of their shame. Rather, they carried themselves with a new perkiness as though conscious of their value as an unusual spectacle. The first two files glanced sideways and grinned in a friendly manner, half the third file followed suit, but the second man looked neither left nor right. He had a scowl on his face, a sneer on his thin lips and he lifted one shoulder in a shrug of contemptuous defiance, delivered, as the watcher realised, not so much towards the curious sightseer, but the world of free men which Mr Harlow represented.

Twisting round in his seat, he watched the little column filing through the Arch of Despair and out of sight through the gun-metal gates which he could not see.

The motorist stepped on the starter and brought the car round in a half-circle. Patiently he manoeuvred the long chassis until it headed back towards Princetown. Tavistock and Ellenbury could wait a day – a week if necessary. For here was a great thought to be shaped and exploited.

His car stopped noiselessly before the Duchy Hotel, and the porter came running down the steps.

'Anything wrong, sir?'

'No. I thought I'd stay another day. Can I have the suite? If not, any room will do.'

The suite was not let, he learnt, and he had his case carried upstairs.

It was then that he decided that Ellenbury, being within

6

driving distance, might come across the moor and save him the tedium of a day spent in Tavistock.

He picked up the telephone and in minutes Ellenbury's anxious voice answered him.

'Come over to Princetown. I'm staying at the Duchy. Don't let people see that you know me. We will get acquainted in the smoke-room after lunch.'

Mr Harlow was eating his frugal lunch at a table overlooking the untidy square in front of the Duchy, when he saw Ellenbury arrive: a small, thin, nervous man, with white hair. Soon after the visitor came down to the big dining-room, gazed quickly round, located Mr Harlow with a start, and sat himself at the nearest table.

The dining-room was sparsely occupied. Two parties that had driven up from Torquay ate talkatively in opposite corners of the room. An elderly man and his stout wife sat at another table, and at a fourth, conveying a curious sense of aloofness, a girl. Women interested Mr Harlow only in so far as they were factors in a problem or the elements of an experiment; but since he must classify all things he saw, he noticed, in his cold-blooded fashion, that she was pretty and therefore unusual; for to him the bulk of humanity bore a marked resemblance to the cheap little suburban streets in which they lived, and the drab centres of commerce where they found their livelihood.

He had once stood at the corner of a busy street in the Midlands and had taken a twelve-hour census of beauty. In that period, though thousands upon thousands hurried past, he had seen one passably pretty girl and two that were not ill-favoured. It was unusual that this girl, who sat sidefaced to him, should be pretty; but she was unusually pretty. Though he could not see her eyes, her visible features were perfect and her complexion was without flaw. Her hair was a gleaming chestnut and he liked the way she used her hands. He believed in the test of hands as a revelation of the mind. Her figure – what was the word? Mr Harlow pursed his lips. His was a cold and exact vocabulary, lacking in

7

floweriness. 'Gracious,' perhaps. He pursed his lips again. Yes, gracious – though why it should be gracious ... He found himself wandering down into the roots of language, and even as he speculated she raised her head slightly and looked at him. In profile she was pleasing enough, but now—

'She is beautiful,' agreed Stratford Harlow with himself, 'but in all probability she has a voice that would drive a man insane.'

Nevertheless, he determined to risk disillusionment. His interest in her was impersonal. Two women, one young, one old, had played important parts in his life; but he could think of women unprejudiced by his experience. He neither liked nor disliked them, any more than he liked or disliked the Farnese vase, which could be admired but had no special utility.

Presently the waiter came to take away his plate.

'Miss Rivers,' said the waiter in a low voice, in answer to his query. 'The young lady came this morning and she's going back to Plymouth by the last train. She's here to see somebody.' He glanced significantly at Mr Harlow, who raised his bushy eyebrows.

'Inside?' he asked, in a low voice.

The waiter nodded.

'Her uncle – Arthur Ingle, the actor chap.'

Mr Harlow nodded. The name was dimly familiar. Ingle? ... Nosegay with a flower drooping out ... and a judge with a cold in his head.

He began to reconstruct from his association of ideas. He had been in court at the Old Bailey and seen the nosegay which every judge carries – a practice which had its beginning in olden times, when a bunch of herbs was supposed to shield his lordship from the taint of Newgate fever. As the judge had laid the nosegay on the ledge, three little pimpernels in the centre had fallen on to the head of the clerk. Now he remembered! Ingle! An ascetic face distorted with fury. Ingle, the actor, who had forged and swindled, and had at last been caught. Mr Stratford Harlow

8

laughed softly; he not only remembered the name but the man; and he had seen him that morning, scowling, and shrugging one shoulder as he slouched past in the field gang. So that was Ingle! And he was an actor.

Mr Harlow had come back especially to Princetown to find out who he was. As he looked up he saw the girl walking quickly from the room and, rising, he strolled out after her, to find the lounge empty. Selecting the most secluded corner, he rang for his coffee and lit a cigar. Presently Ellenbury came in, but for the moment Mr Harlow had other interests. Through the window he saw Miss Rivers walking across the square in the direction of the post office and, rising, he strolled out of the hotel and followed. She was buying stamps when he entered, and it was pleasing to discover that her voice had all the qualities he could desire.

Forty-eight has certain privileges; and can find the openings which would lead to twenty-eight's eternal confusion.

'Good morning, young lady. You're a fellow guest of ours, aren't you?'

He said this with a smile which could be construed as fatherly. She shot a glance at him and her lips twitched. She was too ready to smile, he thought, for this visitation of hers to be wholly sorrowful.

'I lunched at the Duchy, yes, but I'm not staying here. It is a dreadful little town!'

'It has its beauty,' protested Mr Harlow.

He dropped sixpence on the counter, took up a local time-table, waited while the girl's change was counted and fell in beside her as they came out of the office.

'And romance,' he added. 'Take the Feathers Inn. There's a building put up by the labour of French prisoners of war.'

From where they stood only the top of one of the high chimneys of the prison was visible.

She saw him glance in that direction and shake his head.

'The other place, of course, is dreadful – dreadful! I've

been trying to work up my courage to go inside, but somehow I can't.'

'Have you—' She did not finish the question.

'A friend – yes. A very dear friend he was, many years ago, but the poor fellow couldn't go straight. I half promised to visit him, but I dreaded the experience.'

Mr Harlow had no friend in any prison.

She looked at him thoughtfully.

'It isn't really so dreadful. I've been before,' she said, without the slightest embarrassment. 'My uncle is there.'

'Really?' His voice had just the right quantity of sympathy and understanding.

'This is my second visit in four years. I hate it, of course, and I'll be glad when it's over. It is usually rather – trying.'

They were pacing slowly towards the hotel now.

'Naturally it is very dreadful for you. You feel so sorry for the poor fellows—'

She was smiling; he was almost shocked.

'That doesn't distress me very much. I suppose it's a brutal thing to say, but it doesn't. There is no' – she hesitated – 'there is no affection between my uncle and myself, but I'm his only relative and I look after his affairs' – again she seemed at a loss as to how she would explain – 'and whatever money he has. And he's rather difficult to please.'

Mr Harlow was intensely interested; this was an aspect of the visit which he could not have imagined.

'It would be dreadful if I liked him, or if he was fond of me,' she went on, stopping at the foot of the hotel steps. 'As it is, we have a business talk and that is all.'

With a friendly nod she passed into the hotel ahead of him. Mr Harlow stood for a long time in the doorway, looking at nothing, his mind very busy, and then he strolled back to his cooling coffee; and presently fell into discussion about the weather and the crops with the nervous little man who awaited his coming.

They were quite alone now. The car parties had vanished in noisy confusion; the old gentleman and the stout old lady were leaving the hotel on a walking excursion as he had come in.

'Everything all right, Ellenbury?'

'Yes, Mr Harlow,' said the little man eagerly. 'Everything is in perfect shape and trim. I have settled the action that the French underwriters were bringing against the Rata Company, and—'

Suddenly he was stricken to silence. Following the direction of his staring eyes, Mr Harlow also looked out of the window.

Eight convicts were walking down the street in the direction of the railway station; Mr Harlow looked and pointed.

'Not a very pleasant or an agreeable sight,' he said. In his oracular moments his voice was very rich and pleasant. 'Yet one, I think, to which the callous people of Princetown are quite accustomed. These men are being transferred to another prison, I imagine. Do you ever realise what your feelings would be if you had been, say, the leader of that gang, they used to be chained like wild beasts—'

'For God's sake, stop!' said the little man hoarsely. 'Don't talk about it, don't talk about it!'

His trembling hands covered his eyes.

'I had a horror of coming here,' he said, in a voice that was scarcely audible. 'I've never been before ... the car passed that terrible archway and I nearly fainted!'

Mr Harlow, one eye on the door, smiled indulgently. 'You have nothing to fear, my dear Ellenbury,' he said in a paternal voice. 'I have in a sense condoned your felony. In a sense,' he emphasised carefully. 'Whether a judge would take the same view, I do not know. You understand the law better than I. This much is certain; you are free, your debts are paid, the money you stole from your clients has been made good and you have, I think, an income which is, shall we say, satisfactory.'

The little man nodded and swallowed something. He was

white to the lips, and when he tried to lift a glass of water his hand shook so that he had to put it down again.

'I'm very grateful,' he said. 'Very – very grateful. ... I'm sorry – it was rather upsetting.'

'Naturally,' murmured Mr Harlow.

He took a notebook from his pocket, opened it with the greatest deliberation and wrote for five minutes, the little lawyer watching him. When he had finished he tore out the sheet and passed it across the table.

'I want to know all about this man Arthur Ingle,' he said. 'When his sentence expires, where he lives in London or elsewhere, his means and especially his grudge against life. I don't know what it is, but I rather suspect that it is a pretty big one. I should also like to know where his niece is employed. Her name you will find on the paper, with a query mark attached. I want to know who are her friends, what are her amusements, her financial position is very important.'

'I understand.' Ellenbury put the paper carefully in a worn pocket-book. And then, with one of his habitual starts: 'I had forgotten one thing, Mr Harlow,' he said. 'On Monday last I had a visit at my office in Lincoln's Inn Fields from the police.'

He said the last two words apologetically as though he were in some way responsible for the character of his caller. Mr Harlow turned his pale eyes upon his companion, made a long scrutiny of his face before he asked:

'In what connection?'

'I don't know exactly,' said Ellenbury, who had a trick of reproducing at a second's notice all the emotions he described. 'It was rather puzzling.' He screwed up his face into an expression of bewilderment. 'You see, Mr Carlton did not come to any point.'

'Carlton?' demanded Harlow, quickly for him. 'That's the man at the Foreign Office, isn't it?'

Ellenbury nodded.

'Well?'

'It was about the rubber fire. You remember the fire at the United International factory? He wanted to know if Rata had any insurance on the stock that was burnt and of course I told him that as far as I knew, we hadn't.'

'Don't say "we," ' said Mr Harlow gently. 'Say the Rata Syndicate hadn't. You are a lawyer acting for undisclosed principals. Well?'

'That was all,' said Ellenbury. 'He was very vague.'

'He always is vague,' interrupted Harlow with a faint smile, 'and he's always unscrupulous – remember that, Ellenbury. Sub-Inspector James Carlton is the most unscrupulous man that Scotland Yard has ever employed. Some day he will be irretrievably ruined or irretrievably promoted. I have a great admiration for him. I know of no man in the world I rate higher in point of intelligence, acumen and – unscrupulousness! He has a theory which is both admirable and baffling. Which means that he has the right theory. For rectitude is the most baffling of all human qualities, because you never know, if a man is doing right, what he will do next. I think that is almost an epigram, Ellenbury: you had best jot it down, so that if ever you are called upon to write my biography you may have material to lighten its pages.' He looked at his watch. 'I shall be at Park Lane at eleven o'clock on Friday night, and I can give you ten minutes,' he said.

Ellenbury twiddled his fingers unhappily.

'Isn't there a risk – to you, I mean?' he blurted. 'Perhaps I'm stupid, but I can't see why you do ... well, why you take chances. With all your money—'

Mr Harlow leaned back in the cushioned seat, amusement faintly visible in his pale eyes.

'If you had millions what would you do? Retire, of course. Build or buy a beautiful house – and then?'

'I don't know,' said the older man vaguely. 'One could travel ...'

'The English people have two ideas of happiness: one comes from travel, one from staying still! Rushing or rusting! I might marry but I don't wish to marry. I might have a great stable of race-horses, but I detest racing. I might yacht – I loathe the sea. Suppose I want a thrill? I do! The art of living is the art of victory. Make a note of that. Where is happiness in cards, horses, golf, women – anything you like? I'll tell you: in beating the best man to it! That's an Americanism. Where is the joy of mountain climbing, of exploration, of scientific discovery? To do better than somebody else – to go farther, to put your foot on the head of the next best.'

He blew a cloud of smoke through the open window and waited until the breeze had torn the misty gossamer into shreds and nothingness.

'When you're a millionaire you either get inside yourself and become a beast, or get outside of yourself and become a nuisance to your fellows. If you're a Napoleon you will play the game of power, if you're a Leonardo you'll play for knowledge – the stakes hardly matter; it's the game that counts. Accomplishment has its thrill, whether it is hitting a golf ball farther than the next fellow, or strewing the battle fields with the bodies of your enemies. My thrill is harder to get than most people's. I'm a millionaire. Sterling and dollars are my soldiers – I am entitled to frame my own rules of war, conduct my forays in my own way. Don't ask any further questions!'

He waved his hand towards the door and Mr Ellenbury was dismissed; and shortly afterwards his hired car rattled loudly up the hill and past the gates of the jail. Mr Ellenbury studiously turned his face in the opposite direction.

2

SOME EIGHT months later there was an accident on the Thames Embankment. The girl in the yellow raincoat and the man in the black beret were of one accord – they were anxious, for different reasons, to cross the most dangerous stretch of the Embankment in the quickest possible space of time. There was a slight fog which gave promise of being just plain fog before the evening was far advanced. And through the fog percolated an unpleasant drizzle which turned the polished surface of the road into an insurance risk which no self-respecting company would have accepted.

The mudguard of the ancient Ford caught Aileen Rivers just below the left elbow, and she found herself performing a series of unrehearsed pirouettes. Then her nose struck a shining button and she slid romantically to her knees at the feet of a resentful policeman. He lifted her, looked at her, put her aside with great firmness and crossed to where the radiator of the car was staring pathetically up a bent lamp-post.

'What's the idea?' he asked sternly, and groped for his notebook.

The young man in the beret wiped his soiled face with the back of his hand, a gesture which resulted in the further spread of his griminess.

'Was the girl hurt?' he asked quickly.

'Never mind about the girl; let's have a look at your licence.'

Unheeding his authoritative demand, the young man stalked across to where Aileen, embarrassed by the crowd which gathered, was assuring several old ladies that she wasn't hurt. She was standing on her two feet to prove it.

'Waggle your toes about,' suggested a hoarse-voiced woman. 'If they won't move, your back's broke!'

The experiment was not made, for at that moment the tall young man pushed his way to the centre of the curious throng.

'Not hurt, are you?' he asked anxiously. 'I'm awfully sorry – really! Didn't see you till the car was right on top of you.'

A voice from the crowd offered advice and admonition.

'You orter be careful, mister! You might 'a' killed somebody.'

'Tell me your name, won't you?'

He dived into his pocket, found an old envelope and paused.

'Really it isn't necessary. I'm quite unhurt,' she insisted, but he was also insistent.

He jotted down name and address and he had finished writing when the outraged constable melted through the crowd.

'Here!' he said, in a tone in which fierceness and reproach were mingled. 'You can't go running away when I'm talking to you, my friend! Just you stand still and show me that licence of yours.'

'Did you see the blue Rolls?' demanded the young man. 'It was just ahead of me when I hit the lamp-post.'

'Never mind about blue Rolls's,' said the officer in cold exasperation. 'Let me have a look at your licence.'

The young man slipped something out of his pocket and held it in the palm of his hand. It was not unlike a driver's licence and yet it was something else.

'*What's* the idea?' asked the policeman testily.

He snatched the little canvas-backed booklet and opened it, turning his torch on the written words.

'Humph!' he said. 'Sorry, sir.'

'Not at all,' said Sub-Inspector James Carlton of Scotland Yard. 'I'll send somebody down to clear away the mess. Did you see the Rolls?'

'Yes sir, – just in front of you. Petrol tank dented.'

Mr Carlton chuckled.

'Saw that too? I'll remember you, constable. You had better send the girl home in a taxi – no, I'll take her myself.'

Aileen heard the proposal without enthusiasm.

'I much prefer to walk,' she said definitely.

He led her aside from the crowd now being dispersed, authoritatively. And in such privacy as could be obtained momentarily, he revealed himself.

'I am, in fact, a policeman,' he said; and she opened her eyes in wonder.

He did not look like a policeman, even in the fog which plays so many tricks. He had the appearance of a motor mechanic, and not a prosperous one. On his head was a black beret that had seen better days; he wore an old mack reaching to his knees; and the gloves he carried under his arm were black with grease.

'Nevertheless,' he said firmly, as though she had given oral expression to her surprise, 'I am a policeman. But no ordinary policeman. I am an inspector at Scotland Yard – a sub-inspector, it is true, but I have a position to uphold.'

'Why are you telling me all this?'

He had already hailed a taxi and now he opened the door.

'You might object to the escort of an ordinary policeman,' he said airily, 'but my rank is so exalted that you do not need a chaperon.'

She entered the cab between laughter and tears, for her elbow really did hurt more than she was ready to confess.

'Rivers – Aileen Rivers,' he mused, as the cab went cautiously along the Embankment. 'I've got you on the tip of my tongue and at the back of my mind, but I can't place you.'

'Perhaps if you look up my record at Scotland Yard —?' she suggested, with a certain anger at his impertinence.

'I thought of doing that,' he replied calmly; 'but Aileen Rivers?' He shook his head: 'No, I can't place you.'

And of course he had placed her. He knew her as the

niece of Arthur Ingle, sometime Shakespearean actor and now serving five years for an ingenious system of fraud and forgery. But then, he was unscrupulous, as Mr Harlow had said. He had a power of invention which carried him far beyond the creative line, but he was not averse to stooping on the way to the most petty deceptions. And this in spite of the fact that he had been well educated and immense sums had been spent on the development of his mind, so that he might distinguish between right and wrong.

'Fotheringay Mansions.' He fingered his grimy chin. 'How positively exclusive!'

She turned on him in sudden anger.

'I've accepted your escort, Mr—' She paused insultingly.

'Carlton,' he murmured; 'half-brother to the hotel but no relation to the club. And this is fame! You were saying—?'

'I was going to say that I wished you would not talk. You have done your best to kill me this evening; you might at least let me die in peace.'

He peered through the fog-shrouded windows.

'There's an old woman selling chrysanthemums near Westminster Bridge; we might stop and buy you some flowers.' And then, quickly: 'I'm terribly sorry, I won't ask you any questions at all or make any comments upon your plutocratic residence.'

'I don't live there,' she said in self-defence. 'I go there sometimes to see the place is kept in order. It belongs to a – a – relation of mine who is abroad.'

'Monte Carlo?' he murmured. 'And a jolly nice place too! *Rien ne va plus! Faites vos jeux, monsieurs et mesdames!* Personally I prefer San Remo. Blue sky, blue sea, green hills, white houses – everything like a railway poster.' And then he went off at a tangent. 'And talking of blueness, you were lucky not to be hit by the blue Rolls; it was going faster than me, but it has better brakes. I rammed his petrol tank in the fog, but even that didn't make him stop.'

Her lips curled in the darkness.

'A criminal escaping from justice, one thinks? How terribly romantic!'

The young man chuckled.

'One thinks wrong. It was a millionaire on his way to a City banquet. And the only criminal charge I can bring home to him is that he wears large diamond studs in his shirt, which offence is more against my aesthetic taste than the laws of my country, God bless it!'

The cab was slowing, the driver leaning sideways seeking to identify the locality.

'We're here,' said Mr Carlton; opened the door of the taxi while it was still in motion and jumped out.

The machine stopped before the portals of Fotheringay Mansions.

'Thank you very much for bringing me home,' said Aileen primly and politely, and added not without malice: 'I've enjoyed your conversation.'

'You should hear my aunt,' said the young man. 'Her line of talk is sheer poetry!'

He watched her until she was swallowed in the gloom, and returned to the cab.

'Scotland Yard,' he said laconically; 'and take a bit of a risk, O son of Nimshi.'

The cabman took the necessary risk and arrived without hurt at the gloomy entrance of police headquarters. Jim Carlton waved a brotherly greeting to the sergeant at the desk, took the stairs two at a time, and came to his own little room. As a rule he was not particularly interested in his personal appearance, but now, glancing at the small mirror which decorated the upturned top of a washstand, he uttered a groan.

He was busy getting the grease from his face when the melancholy face of Inspector Elk appeared in the doorway.

'Going to a party?' he asked gloomily.

'No,' said Jim through the lather; 'I often wash.'

Elk sniffed, seated himself on the edge of a hard chair, searched his pockets slowly and thoroughly.

'It's in the inside pocket of my jacket,' spluttered Carlton. 'Take one; I've counted 'em.'

Elk sighed heavily as he took out the long leather case, and, selecting a cigar, lit it.

'Seegars are not what they was when I was a boy,' he said, gazing at the weed disparagingly. 'For sixpence you could get a real Havana. Over in New York everybody smokes cigars. But then, they pay the police a livin' wage; they can afford it.'

Mr Carlton looked over his towel.

'I've never known you to buy a cigar in your life,' he said deliberately. 'You can't get them cheaper than for nothing!'

Inspector Elk was not offended.

'I've smoked some good cigars in my time,' he said. 'Over in the Public Prosecutor's office in Mr Gordon's days – he was the fellow that smashed the Frogs – him and me, that is to say,' he corrected himself carefully.

'The Frogs? Oh, yes, I remember. Mr Gordon had good cigars, did he?'

'Pretty good,' said Elk cautiously. 'I wouldn't say yours was worse, but it's not better.' And then, without a change of voice: 'Have you pinched Stratford Harlow?'

Jim Carlton made a grimace of disgust.

'Tell me something I can pinch him for,' he invited.

'He's worth fifteen millions according to accounts,' said Elk. 'No man ever got fifteen million honest.'

Jim Carlton turned a white, wet face to his companion.

'He inherited three from his father, two from one aunt, one from another. The Harlows have always been a rich family, and in the last decade they've graded down to maiden aunts. He had a brother in America who left him eight million dollars.'

Elk sighed and scratched his thin nose.

'He's in Ratas too,' he said complainingly.

'Of course he's in Ratas!' scoffed Jim. 'Ellenbury hides him, but even if he didn't, there's nothing criminal in Rata.

And supposing he was openly in it, that would be no offence.'

'Oh!' said Elk, and by that 'Oh!' indicated his tentative disagreement.

There was nothing furtive or underhand about the Rata Syndicate. It was registered as a public company, and had its offices in Westshire House, Old Broad Street, in the City of London, and its New York office on Wall Street. The Rata Syndicate published a balance sheet and employed a staff of ten clerks, three of whom gained further emoluments by acting as directors of the company, under the chairmanship of a retired colonel of infantry. The capital was a curiously small one, but the resources of the syndicate were enormous. When Rata cornered rubber, cheques amounting to five millions sterling passed outward through its banking accounts; in fact every cent involved in that great transaction appeared in the books except the fifty thousand dollars that somebody paid to Lee Hertz and his two friends.

Lee arrived from New York on a Friday afternoon. On the Sunday morning the United Continental Rubber Company's stores went up in smoke. Nearly eighteen thousand tons of rubber were destroyed in that well-organised conflagration, and rubber jumped 80 per cent. in twenty-four hours and 200 per cent. in a week. For the big reserves that kept the market steady had been wiped out in the twinkling of an eye, to the profit of Rata Incorporated.

Said the New York Headquarters to Scotland Yard:

Lee Hertz, Jo Klein and Philip Serrett well known fire bugs believed to be in London stop See record NY 9514 mailed you October 7 for description stop Possibility you may connect them United Continental fire.

By the time Scotland Yard located Lee he was in Paris in his well-known rôle of American Gentleman Seeing the Sights.

'It doesn't look right to me,' said Elk, puffing luxuriously at the cigar. 'Here's Rata buys rubber with not a ghost of a chance of its rising. And suddenly, biff! A quarter of the reserve stock in this country is burnt out, and naturally prices and shares rise. Rata's been buying 'em for months. Did they know that the United was going west?'

'I thought it might have been an accident,' said Jim, who had never thought anything of the sort.

'Accident my grandmother's right foot!' said Elk, without heat. 'The stores were lit up in three places – the salvage people located the petrol. A man answering the description of Jo Klein was drinking with the night watchman the day before, and that watchman swears he never saw this Jo bird again, but he's probably lying. The lower classes lie easier than they drink. Ten millions, and if Harlow's behind Rata, he made more than that on the rubber deal. Buying orders everywhere! Toronto, Rio, Calcutta – every loose bit of rubber lifted off the market. Then comes the fire, and up she goes! All I got to say is—'

The telephone bell rang shrilly at that second, and Jim Carlton picked up the receiver.

'Somebody wants you, Inspector,' said the exchange clerk.

There was a click, an interval of silence, and then a troubled voice asked:

'Can I speak to Mr Carlton?'

'Yes, Miss Rivers.'

'Oh, it's you, is it?' There was a flattering relief in the voice. 'I wonder if you would come to Fotheringay Mansions, No. 63?'

'Is anything wrong?' he asked quickly.

'I don't know, but one of the bedroom doors is locked, and I'm sure there's nobody in there.'

3

THE GIRL was standing in the open doorway of the flat as the two men stepped from the elevator. She seemed a little disconcerted at the sight of Inspector Elk, but Jim Carlton introduced him as a friend and obliterated him as a factor with one comprehensive gesture.

'I suppose I ought to have sent for the local police, only there are – well, there are certain reasons why I shouldn't,' she said.

Somehow Jim had never thought she could be so agitated. The discovery had evidently thrown her off her balance, and she was hardly lucid when she explained.

'I come here to collect my uncle's letters,' she said. 'He's abroad ... his name is Jackson,' she said breathlessly. 'And every Thursday I have a woman in to clean up the flat. I can't afford the time; I'm working in an office.'

They had left Elk staring at an engraving in the corridor, and it was an opportunity to make matters a little easier, if at first a little more uncomfortable, for her.

'Miss Rivers, your uncle is Arthur Ingle,' said Jim kindly, and she went very red. 'It is quite understandable that you shouldn't wish to advertise the fact, but I thought I'd tell you I knew, just to save you a great deal of unnecessary—' He stopped and seemed at a loss.

' "Lying" is the word you want,' she said frankly. 'Yes, Arthur Ingle lived here, but he lived here in the name of Jackson. Did you know that?' she asked anxiously.

He nodded.

'That's the door.' She pointed.

The flat was of an unusual construction. There was a very large dining-room with a low-timbered roof and panelled walls, from which led three doors – one to the kitchenette, the other two, she explained, to Arthur Ingle's bedroom and a spare apartment which he used as a lumber room. It was the door of the lumber room which she indicated.

Jim tried the handle; the door was fast. Stooping down he peered through the keyhole and had a glimpse of an open window through which the yellow fog showed.

'Are these doors usually left open?'

'Always,' she said emphatically. 'Sometimes the cleaning woman comes before I return. Tonight she is late and I'm rather early.'

'Where does that door lead?'

'To the kitchen.'

She went in front of him into the tiny room. It was spotlessly clean and had one window, flush with that which he had seen through the keyhole of the next room. He looked down into a bottomless void, but just beneath was a narrow parapet. He swung one leg across the sill, only to find his arm held in a frenzied grip by the girl.

'You mustn't go, you'll be killed!' she gasped and he laughed at her, not ill pleased, for the risk was practically *nil*.

'I've got a pretty high regard for me,' he said, and in another instant he had swung clear, gripped the lower sash of the second window and had pulled himself into the room.

He could see nothing except the dim outlines of three trunks stacked one on top of the other. He switched on the light and turned to survey the confusion. Old boxes and trunks which, he guessed, had been piled in some order, were dragged into the centre of the room to allow the free operation of the vanished burglar. Recessed into the wall, thus cleared, was a safe the door of which was open. On the floor beneath was a rough circle of metal burnt from the door – it was still hot when he touched it – by the small blowlamp that the burglar had left behind him.

He unlocked the door of the room and admitted Elk and the girl.

'That's good work,' said Elk, whose detached admiration for the genius of law-breakers was at least sincere. 'Safe's empty! Not so much as a cigarette card left behind. Good work! Toby Haggitt or Lew Yakobi – they're the only two men in London that could have done it.'

The girl was gazing wide-eyed at the 'good work'. She was very pale, Jim noticed, and misread the cause.

'What was in the safe?' he asked.

She shook her head.

'I don't know – I didn't even know that there was a safe in the room. He will be terrible about this!'

Carlton knew the 'he' was the absent Ingle.

'He won't know for some time, anyway—' he began, but she broke in upon his reassurance.

'Next week,' she said; 'he is being released on Wednesday.'

Elk scratched his chin thoughtfully.

'Somebody knew that,' he said; 'he hadn't a partner either.'

Arthur Ingle was indeed a solitary worker. His frauds had been unsuspected even by such friends as he had in his acting days – for they had covered a period of twelve years before his arrest and conviction. To the members of his company he was known as a bad paymaster and an unscrupulous manager; none imagined that this clever player of character parts was 'Lobber & Syne, Manufacturing Jewellers, of Clerkenwell,' and other *aliases* that produced him such golden harvests.

'It was no fault of yours,' said Jim Carlton; and she submitted to a gentle pat on the shoulder. 'There's no sense in worrying about it.'

Elk was examining the blowlamp under the electric light.

'Bet it's Toby,' he said, and walked to the window. 'That's his graft. He'd make a cat burglar look like a wool-eatin' kitten! Parapets are like the Great West Road to Toby – he'd stop to manicure his nails on three inches of rotten sandstone.'

The identity of the burglar worried Jim less than it did the girl. He had the brain of a lightning calculator. A hundred aspects of the crime, a hundred possibilities and explanations flickered through his mind and none completely satisfied him.

Unless—

The Splendid Harlow was on the way to becoming an obsession. There was no immense sum of money to be made from discovering the secrets of a convicted swindler. That there was money in the safe he did not for one moment believe. Ingle was not the type of criminal which hid its wealth in safes. He credited him with a dozen banking accounts in fictitious names, and each holding money on deposit.

They went back into the panelled dining-room. The apartment interested Jim, for here was every evidence of luxury and refinement. The flat must have cost thousands of pounds to furnish. And then he remembered that Arthur Ingle had been convicted on three charges. Evidence in a number of others, which must have produced enormous profits, was either missing or of too shaky a character to produce. This apartment represented coups more successful than those for which Arthur Ingle had been convicted.

'Do you know your uncle very well?'

She shook her head.

'I knew him better many years ago,' she said, 'when he was an actor, before he – well, before he got rich! I am his only living relation.' She raised her head, listening. Somebody had knocked at the outer door.

'It may be the charwoman,' she said, and went along the passage to open the door.

A man was standing on the mat outside, tall, commanding, magnificent in his well-cut evening clothes. His snowy linen blazed and twinkled with diamonds; the buttons on his white waistcoat were a-glitter.

It was part of the primitive in the man, so that she saw nothing vulgar in the display. But something within her shrank under his pale gaze. She had a strange and inexplicable sensation of being in the presence of a power beyond earthly control. She was crushed by the sense of his immense superiority. So she might have felt had she found herself confronted by a tiger.

'My name is Harlow – we met on Dartmoor,' he said, and showed a line of even teeth in a smile. 'May I come in?'

She could not speak in her astonishment, but somebody answered for her.

'Come in, Harlow,' drawled Jim Carlton's voice. 'I'd love to have your first impression of Dartmoor; is it really as snappy as people think?'

4

MR HARLOW'S attitude towards this impertinent man struck the girl as remarkable. It was mild, almost benevolent; he seemed to regard James Carlton as a good joke. And he was the great Harlow! She had learnt that at Princetown.

You could not work in the City without hearing of Harlow, his coups and successes. Important bankers spoke of him with bated breath. His money was too liquid for safety: it flowed here and there in floods that were more often than not destructive. Sometimes it would disappear into subterranean caverns, only to gush forth in greater and more devastating volume to cut new channels through old cultivations and presently to recede, leaving havoc and ruin behind.

And of course she had heard of the police station. When Mr Harlow interested himself in the public weal he did so thoroughly and unconventionally. His letters to the press on the subject of penology were the best of their kind that have appeared in print. He pestered Ministers and Commissioners with his plans for a model police station, and when his enthusiasm was rebuffed he did what no philanthropist, however public-minded, has ever done before.

He bought a freehold plot in Evory Street (which is not a stone's throw from Park Lane), built his model police headquarters at the cost of two hundred thousand pounds, and presented the building to the police commissioners. It was a model police office in every respect. The men's quarters above the station were the finest of their kind in the world. Even the cells had the quality of comfort, though they contained the regulation plank bed. This gift was a nine days' wonder. Topical revues had their jokes about it; the cartoonists flung their gibes at the Government upon the happening.

The City had ceased to think of him as eccentric, they called him 'sharp' and contrasted him unfavourably with his father. They were a little afraid of him. His money was too fluid for stability.

He nodded smilingly at Jim Carlton, fixed the unhappy Elk with a glance, and then:

'I did not know that you and my friend Carlton were acquainted.' And then, in a changed tone: 'I hope I am not *de trop*?'

His voice, his attitude said as plainly as words could express: 'I presume this is a police visitation due to the notorious character of your uncle?'

The girl thought this. Jim knew it.

'There has been a burglary here and Miss Rivers called us in,' he said.

Harlow murmured his regrets and sympathy.

'I congratulate you upon having secured the shrewdest officer in the police force.' He addressed the girl blandly. 'And I congratulate the police force' – he looked at Jim – 'upon detaching you from the Foreign Office – you were wasted there, Mr Carlton, if I may be so impertinent as to express an opinion.'

'I am still in the Foreign Office,' said Jim. 'This is spare-time work. Even policemen are entitled to their amusements. And how did you like Dartmoor?'

The Splendid Harlow smiled sadly.

'Very impressive, very tragic,' he said. 'I am referring of course to Princetown where I spent a couple of nights.'

Aileen was waiting to hear the reason for the call; even through her distress and foreboding she was curious to learn what whim had brought this super-magnate to the home of a convict.

He looked slowly from her to the men and again Jim interpreted his wishes; he glanced at Elk and walked with him into the lumber room.

'It occurred to me,' said Mr Harlow, 'that I might be in a position to afford you some little help. My name may not be wholly unknown to you; I am Mr Stratford Harlow.'

She nodded.

'I knew that,' she said.

'They told you at the Duchy, did they?' It seemed that he was relieved that she had identified him.

'Mine is rather a delicate errand, but it struck me – I have found myself thinking about you many times since we met – that possibly ... I might be able to find a good position for you. Your situation, if you will forgive my saying as much, is a little tragic. Association with – er – criminals or people with criminal records has a drugging effect even upon the finest nature.'

She smiled.

'In other words, Mr Harlow,' she said quietly, 'you're under the impression I'm rather badly off and that you would like to make life easier for me?'

He beamed at this.

'Exactly,' he said.

'It is very kind of you – most kind,' she said, and meant it. 'But I have a very good job in a lawyer's office.'

He inclined his head graciously.

'Mr Stebbings has been very good to me—'

'Mr —?' His head jerked on one side. 'Stebbings – of Stebbings, Field & Farrow – surely not! They were my lawyers until a few years ago.'

She knew this also.

'Quite good people, though a little old-fashioned,' he said. 'Then of course you have heard Mr Stebbings speak of me?'

'Only once,' she confessed. 'He is a very reticent man and never talks about his clients.'

Harlow bit his lip in thought.

'An excellent fellow! I have often wondered whether I was wrong in taking my affairs from him. I wish you would mention that to him when you see him. I understood you were working in the office of the New Library Syndicate?'

She smiled at this.

'It's curious you should say that; their offices are in Lincoln's Inn Fields, but next door.'

'Ah!' he said. 'I see how the mistake arose,' and added quickly: 'A friend of mine who knows you saw you going into – er – an office; and obviously made a mistake.'

He did not tell her who was their mutual friend, and she was not sufficiently interested to inquire.

This time the knock at the door was more pronounced.

'Will you excuse me?' she said. 'That is my cleaner, and she is rather inclined to tell me her troubles. I may keep you waiting a little while.'

She left him and he heard the sounds of a door opening, as Jim Carlton and Elk came back into the dining-room.

'A very charming young lady that,' said Mr Harlow.

'Very,' said Jim shortly.

'Women do not interest me greatly' – the Splendid Harlow picked a tiny thread of cotton from his immaculate coat and dropped it on the floor. 'They think along lines which I find it difficult to follow. They are emotional, too – swayed by momentary fears and scruples....'

The sound of voices in the passage, one high-pitched and complaining:

'... what with the fog and everything, miss, it's lucky I'm here at all....'

A shabby figure passed the open door, followed by Aileen.

'I suppose you don't know Ingle, Mr Harlow?' Jim was

examining the photograph on the mantelpiece. 'A long-firm swindler; clever, but with a kink even in his kinkiness! Believes in revolution and all that sort of thing ... blood and guillotines and tumbrils; the whole box of tricks—'

Something made him look round.

Mr Stratford Harlow was standing in the centre of the room, gripping the edge of a small table to keep him upright. His face was white and haggard and drawn; and in his pale eyes was a look of horror such as Jim Carlton had never seen in the face of a man. Elk sprang forward and caught him as he swayed and led him to a big settee. Into this Stratford Harlow sank and leaning forward, covered his face with his hands.

'Oh, my God!' he said as he rocked slowly from side to side and fell in a heap on the ground.

The colossus had fainted.

5

'A LITTLE heart trouble,' said Mr Harlow, smiling as he set down the glass of water. 'I'm terribly sorry to have given you so much trouble, Miss Rivers. I haven't had an attack in years.'

He was still pale, but such was his extraordinary self-control that the hand that put down the glass was without a tremor.

'Phew!' He dabbed his forehead with a silk handkerchief and rose steadily to his feet.

Elk was engaged in the prosaic task of brushing the dust stains from his knees and looked up.

'You'd better let me take you home, Mr Harlow,' he said.

Stratford Harlow shook his head.

'That is quite unnecessary – quite,' he said. 'I have my

car at the door and a remedy for all such mental disturbances as these! And it is not a drug!' he smiled.

Nevertheless, Elk went with him to the car.

'Will you tell my chauffeur to drive to the Charing Cross power station?' was the surprising request; and long after the car had moved off in the fog Elk stood on the sidewalk, wondering what business took this multi-millionaire to such a venue.

They evidently knew Mr Harlow at the power station and they at any rate saw nothing remarkable in his visit. The engineer, who was smoking at the door, stood back to let him walk into the great machinery hall, and placed a stool for him. And there for half an hour he sat, and the droning of the dynamos and the whirr and thud of the great engines were sedatives and anodynes to his troubled mind.

Here he had come before, to think out great schemes, which developed best in this atmosphere. The power and majesty of big wheels, the rhythm of the driving belts as they sagged and rose, the shaded lights above the marble switchboards, the noisy quiet of it all, stimulated him as nothing else could. Here he found the illusion of irresistibility that attuned so perfectly to his own mood; the inevitable effects of the inevitable causes. The sense that he was standing near the very heart of power was an inspiration. This lofty hall was a very home of the gods to him.

Half an hour, an hour, passed, and then he rose with a catch of his breath, and a slow smile lit the big face.

'Thank you, Harry, thank you.'

He shook the attendant's hand and left something that crinkled in the hard palm of the workman. A few minutes later he drove through brilliantly illuminated Piccadilly Circus and could offer a friendly nod to the flickering and flashing lights whose birth he had seen and whose very brilliance was a homage to the steel godhead.

To be thoroughly understood, Mr Stratford Harlow must be known.

There had been five members of the Harlow family when Stratford Selwyn Mortimer Harlow was born, and they were all immensely rich. His mother died a week later, his father when he was aged three, leaving the infant child to the care of his Aunt Mercy, a spinster who was accounted, even by her charitable relatives, as 'strange'. The boy was never sent to school, for his health was none of the best and he had his education at the hands of his aunt. An enormously rich woman with no interest in life, she guarded her charge jealously. Family interference drove her to a frenzy. The one call that her two sisters paid her, when the boy was seven, ended in a scene on which Miss Alice, the younger, based most of her conversation for years afterwards.

The main result of the quarrel between Miss Mercy and her maiden sisters was that she shut up Kravelly Hall and removed, with her maid Mrs Edwins, to a little cottage at Teignmouth. Here she lived unmolested by her relatives for seven years. She then went to Scarborough for three years and thence to Bournemouth. Regularly every month she wrote to her two sisters and her bachelor brother in New York; and the terminology of the letters did not vary by so much as a comma:

> Miss Mercy Harlow presents her compliments and begs to state that The Boy is in Good Health and is receiving adequate tuition in the essential subjects together with a sound instruction in the tenets of the Protestant Faith.

She had engaged a tutor, a bearded young man from Oxford University (she deigned to mention this fact to her brother, with whom she had not quarrelled), whose name was Marling. There came to the ears of Aunt Alice a story which called into question the fitness of Mr Marling to mould the plastic mind of youth. A mild scandal at Oxford. Miss Alice felt it her duty to write, and after a long interval had a reply:

> Miss Mercy Harlow begs to thank Miss Alice Harlow for her communication and in reply begs to state that she has conducted a very thorough and searching enquiry into the charges preferred

33

against Mr Saul Marling (B.A. Oxon) and is satisfied that Mr Marling acted in the most *honourable* manner, and has done nothing with which he may reproach himself or which renders him unfit to direct the studies of The Boy.

This happened a year before Miss Mercy's death. When nature took its toll and she passed to her Maker, Miss Alice hastened to Bournemouth and in a small and secluded cottage near Christchurch found a big and solemn young man of twenty-three, dressed a little gawkily in black. He was tearless; and indeed, his aunt suspected, almost cheerful at the prospect of being freed from Miss Mercy's drastic management.

The bearded tutor had left (Mrs Edwins, the maid, tearfully explained) a fortnight before the passing of Miss Mercy.

'And if he hadn't gone,' said Miss Alice with tight lips, 'I should have made short work of him! The Boy has been suppressed! He hasn't a word to say for himself!'

A council was held, including the family lawyer, who was making his first acquaintance with Stratford. It was agreed that The Boy should have a flat in Park Lane and the companionship of an elder man who combined a knowledge of the world with a leaning towards piety. Such was found in the Rev. John Barthurst, M.A., an ex-naval chaplain. Mrs Edwins was pensioned off and the beginning of Stratford's independent life was celebrated with a dinner and a visit to *Charley's Aunt*, through which roaring farce he sat with a stony face.

The tutelage lasted the best part of a year; and then the quiet young man suddenly came to life, dismissed his worldly and pious companion with a cheque for a thousand pounds, summoned Mrs Edwins to be his housekeeper; and bought and reconstructed the Duke of Greenhart's house in Park Lane.

And thenceforward Mr Harlow's name began to appear in the records of important transactions. Family fortunes dropped into his lap. Miss Mercy had been fabulously rich and had left him every penny of her fortune, with the exception of '£100 to Lucy Edwins in recognition of her faithful service, realising that she will not regard this sum as inadequate in view of the great service I rendered to her.' Then Miss Henrietta died; and when the death duties were paid there was the greater part of two millions. Miss Alice left more. The bachelor uncle in New York died a comparative pauper, leaving a beggarly six hundred thousand.

Mr Harlow's house was a rather ugly three-storey building which occupied a small island site, possibly the most valuable in Park Lane, though the actual entrance was not in that exclusive thoroughfare, but in the side street. He opened the door with a key and walked into the hall. The door to the library faced him. There were some letters on the table, which he scanned through rapidly, opening only one. It was from Ellenbury; and just then Mr Harlow was annoyed with Ellenbury; he had supplied erroneous information about Aileen Rivers, and had made him look a fool.

He read the letter carefully, and then dropped it in the fire and watched it turn black.

'A useful man, but a thought too anxious. It was a mistake perhaps to keep him so taut. He must be let down,' Mr Harlow decided. A little of his own confidence must be infused into his helper. Too great a desire to please, too present a fear of failure: those were Ellenbury's weaknesses.

He pressed an ivory bell on his desk, sat down, reached to the wall, slid back a panel and took out a small black bottle, a siphon and a glass. He poured out barely more whisky than was enough to cover the bottom of the tumbler, and filled it to the top with soda-water. The glass was half-empty when Mrs Edwins, his housekeeper, came in without knocking. A tall, yellow-faced woman, with burning black eyes, she showed nothing of the slowness or decrepitude that might have been expected in a woman near seventy.

'You rang?'

Miss Mercy's maid of other days had a voice as sharp and clear as a bugle note.

She stood before the desk, her hands behind her, her eyes fixed on his.

'Yes,' he said, turning over his letters once more. 'Is everything all right?'

'Everything.'

Like a bugle note and with some of a bugle's stridency.

'Couldn't we keep a servant in the house?' she asked. 'The hours are a little too long for me. I didn't get to bed until one o'clock yesterday, and I had to be up at seven to let them in.'

It was a curious fact that no servants slept at No. 704, Park Lane. There was not a house of its size, or an establishment of such pretensions, in all the country where every servant slept out. Mr Harlow's excuse to his friends was that the room space was too valuable for servants, but he denied this by hiring an expensive house in Charles Street for their accommodation.

'No, I don't think it is necessary,' he said, pursing his lips. 'I thought you understood that.'

'I might die, or be taken ill in the night,' said Mrs Edwins dispassionately, 'and then where would you be?'

He smiled.

'It would be rather a case of where would you be, I think!' he said in excellent humour. 'Nothing has happened?'

She considered her answer before she replied.

'Somebody called, that was all,' she said, 'but I'll tell you about that afterwards.'

He was amused.

'A good many people call. Very well – be mysterious!'

He got up from his chair and walked out of the room, and she followed. There was a tiny elevator in the hall, big enough for two, but she declined this conveyance.

'I'll walk,' she said, and he laughed softly.

'You were complaining about feeling tired just now,' he retorted as he closed the grille before the little lift.

He pressed the top button, the elevator moved swiftly and noiselessly upwards and came at last to a stop on the third floor, where he stepped out to a square-carpeted landing from which led two doors. Here he waited, humming softly to himself, until the woman came in sight round the bend of the stairs.

'You're an athlete,' he said pleasantly and, jerking out a pocket-chain, selected a small key and opened the door on the left.

It was a big and artistically furnished apartment, lit from the cornice by concealed light and from the floor by two red-shaded lamps. In one corner of the room was an ornate wooden bed of red lacquer decorated with Chinese paintings in gold. At a small Empire desk near one of the windows, which were heavily curtained, sat a man. He was almost as tall as Stratford Harlow; and the features which would have arrested the attention of a stranger were his big, dome-shaped forehead and the long golden-yellow beard which, in spite of his age – and he must have been as old as Harlow himself – was untinged with grey.

He was reading, one thin hand on his cheek, his eyes fixed upon the book that lay on the desk, and not until Mr Harlow spoke did he look up.

'Hallo, Marling!' said Stratford Harlow gently.

The man leaned back in his chair, closed the book, mechanically marking his place with a thin tortoise-shell paper-knife.

'Good evening,' he said simply.

'Time you had your walk, isn't it?'

There was a second door in the room and towards this Mr Harlow glanced.

'Yes, I suppose it is,' said the man, and rose.

He wore a short dressing-jacket of dark blue velvet; his feet were encased in red morocco slippers. His glance strayed back to the closed book as though he were reluctant to have his reading interrupted.

'The Odes of Horace,' he said; 'an English translation, but full of errors.'

'Yes, yes,' smiled Mr Harlow. 'It's rather late for Horace.'

The woman was standing by the door, stiffly erect, her hands folded in front of her, her dark eyes on her master.

'Do you know who you are, my friend?' he asked.

The bearded man put his white hand to his forehead.

'I am Saul Marling, a graduate of Balliol,' he said.

Mr Harlow nodded.

'And – anything else?' he asked.

Again the hand went up to the dome-shaped forehead.

'I forget . . . how absurd! It was something I saw, wasn't it?' he asked anxiously.

'Something you saw,' agreed Mr Harlow, 'just before Miss Mercy died.'

The other heaved a sigh.

'She died very suddenly. She was very kind to me in all my little troubles. Awfully suddenly! She used to sit on the chair talking to you, and then one night after dinner she fell down.'

'On the floor,' nodded Mr Harlow, almost cheerfully. 'But you saw something, didn't you?' he encouraged. 'A little bottle and some blue stuff. Wake up, Marling! You remember the little bottle and the blue stuff?'

The man shook his head.

'Not clearly . . . that was before you and Mrs Edwins took me away. I drank the white powders – they fizzed like a seidlitz powder – and then . . .'

'To the country,' smiled Harlow. 'You were ill, my poor old fellow, and we had to prescribe something to quieten you. You're all right?'

'My head is a little confused—' began the man, but Harlow laughed, caught him almost affectionately by the arm and, opening the narrow door, led his companion up a flight of steep stairs. At the top of this was another door, which Mr Harlow unlocked. They were on the roof of Greenhart House, a wide, flat expanse of asphalt confined within a breast-high parapet. For half an hour they walked up and down arm-in-arm, the bigger man talking all the time.

The fog was thick, the street lamps showed themselves below as patches of dull yellow luminosity.

'Cold? I told you to put on your scarf, you stupid chap!' Mr Harlow was good-humoured even in his annoyance. 'Come along, we'll go down.'

In the room below he fastened the door and gazed approvingly round the comfortable apartment. He took up one of the eight volumes that lay on a table. They still wore the publishers' wrappers and had arrived that day.

'Reading maketh a full man – you will find the Augustan histories a little heavy even for a graduate of Oxford, eh? Good night, Marling – sleep well.'

He locked the door and went out on to the landing with Mrs Edwins. Her hard eyes were fixed on his face, and until he spoke she was silent.

'He's quite all right,' he said.

'Is he?' Her harsh voice was disagreeable. 'How can he be all right if he's reading *and* writing?'

'Writing?' he asked quickly. 'What?'

'Oh, just stuff about the Romans, but it reads sensible.'

Mr Harlow considered this frowningly.

'That means nothing. He gives no trouble.'

'No,' she said shortly. 'I get worried,' she went on, 'but he's quiet. Who is Mr Carlton?'

Harlow drew a quick breath.

'Has he been here?'

She nodded.

'Yes – this afternoon. He asked me if I was Miss Mercy's old maid – she must have died soon after he was born.'

'He's older than that – well?'

'I thought it was queer, but he said he'd been asked to trace Mr Saul Marling.'

'By whom?'

She confessed her ignorance with a look.

'I don't know; but it was a proper inquiry. He showed me the papers. They were from Eastbourne. I told him

39

Marling was dead. "Where?" he said. "In South America," I told him.'

'Pernambuco,' emphasised Mr Harlow, 'in the plague epidemic. Humph! Clever . . . and unscrupulous. Thank you.'

She watched him pass into the elevator and drop out of sight, then she went into the second room that opened from the landing. This too, was pleasantly furnished. Turning on the lights she sat down and opened a big chintz bag. From this she took an unfinished stocking and adjusted her knitting needles. And as her nimble fingers moved, so did her lips.

'Pernambuco – in the plague epidemic,' she was saying.

6

AILEEN RIVERS lived in Bloomsbury, which had the advantage of being near her work. She had spent a restless night, and the day that followed had been full of vexation. Mr Stebbings, her immediate chief, was away nursing a cold; and his junior partner, with whom she was constantly brought into contact that day, was a tetchy and disagreeable man, with a habit of mislaying important documents and blaming the person who happened to be most handy for their disappearance.

At six o'clock in the evening she locked up her desk with a sigh of thankfulness, looking forward to a light dinner and an early bedtime. Through her window she had seen the car drawn up by the kerb, and at first had thought it was waiting for a client, so that she was a little surprised, and by no means pleased, when, as she came down the steps of the old-fashioned house where the office was situate, a young man crossed the broad sidewalk towards her and lifted his hat.

'Oh, *you*!' she said in some dismay.

'Me, or I, as the case may be; I'm not quite certain which,' said Jim Carlton. 'And your tone is offensive,' he said sternly. 'By rights Elk or I should have been interviewing you at all sorts of odd hours during the day.'

'But what on earth can I tell you?' she asked, exasperated. 'You know everything about the burglary – I suppose that is what you mean?'

'That is what I mean,' said Jim. 'It is very evident that you know nothing about policemen. You imagine, I suppose, that Scotland Yard says "Hallo, there's been a burglary in Victoria. How interesting! Nobody knows anything about it, so we'll let the matter drop." You're wrong!'

'I'm much too hungry to talk.'

'So I guessed,' he said. 'There is an unpretentious restaurant at King's Cross, where the *sole bonne femme* is worthy only of the pure of heart.'

She hesitated.

'Very well,' she said a little ungraciously. 'Is that your car? How funny!'

'There's nothing funny about my car,' he said with dignity, 'and it is not my car. I borrowed it.'

It was a clear night of stars and there was a touch of frost in the air and, although she would not have admitted as much for untold wealth, she enjoyed the short run that brought them to the side entrance of a large restaurant filled with people in varying stages of gastronomic enjoyment.

'I have booked a table,' he said, piloting her through an avenue of working jaws to a secluded corner of the annexe.

The atmosphere of the place was very satisfying. The pink table-lamps had a soothing effect, and she could examine him at her leisure. In truth it had been one of the sources of irritation of that very unhappy day that she could not quite remember what he looked like. She knew that he was not repulsive, and had a misty idea that he was rather good-looking, but that his nose was too short. It proved on inspection to be of a reasonable length. His eyes were blue

41

and he was a little older than she had thought. Half her disrespect was based on the illusion of his youth.

'Now ask all your horrid questions,' she said as she took off her gloves.

'Number one,' he began. 'What did Harlow offer you when I so discreetly withdrew last night?'

'That has nothing to do with the burglary,' she answered promptly. 'But as it wasn't very important, I will tell you. He offered me a position.'

'Where?' he asked quickly.

She shook her head.

'I don't know. We didn't get as far as that; I told him I was perfectly happy with Mr Stebbings – who, by the way, used to be the lawyer of the Harlow family.'

'Did you tell him that?'

He thrust his head forward eagerly.

'Why, no – he told me, though of course I knew,' she said. 'He knew, the moment I mentioned Stebbings's name.'

'Was he impressed?' he asked after a pause and she laughed.

'How ridiculous you are! Seriously, Mr —'she paused insultingly.

'Carlton,' he murmured; 'half-brother to the hotel but no relation to the club.'

'You worked that one last night,' she said.

'And I shall work it every night you pretend to forget my name! Anyway, it is a confession of crass ignorance which no modern young woman can afford to make. I am one of the most famous men in London.'

'I think I've heard you say that before,' she said mendaciously. 'Now tell me seriously, Mr Carlton—'

'Got it!' he murmured.

'What do you want to know about the burglary?'

'Nothing,' was the shameless reply. 'As a matter of fact, I have saved you a great deal of trouble by supplying headquarters with all the details they need. Your uncle emerges tomorrow; do you know that?'

42

'Tomorrow?' she said, with a pang of apprehension.

'And Elk is going to meet him and take some of the sting out of his anger. I suppose he will be very angry?'

'He'll be furious,' said the girl, troubled. And then, with a quick sigh, 'I'll be awfully glad when he has "emerged," as you call it. He allows me two pounds a week for my trouble, but I can well spare that.'

'Arthur Ingle ought to be ashamed of himself to drag you into the light which shines so brightly upon the unjust,' he said. 'There is only one thing I want to know about him, and perhaps you can tell me – was your uncle a great speculator?'

'I don't think so. But really I don't know. He never spoke to me about any investments. Is that what you mean?'

'That is just what I mean,' said Jim.

He found it difficult to put the question without offence.

'You've had interviews with him and I dare say you've discussed his business to some extent. I shouldn't ask you to betray his confidence and I don't suppose for one minute you will. Did he ever talk about foreign gilt-edged investments?'

She was shaking her head before he finished the question.

'Never,' she said. 'I don't think he knows much about them. I remember the first time I saw him at Dartmoor he told me he didn't believe in putting money in shares. Of course, I'm well aware he has money, but you know that, too, and I suppose it is stolen money that he's—'

'Cached – yes,' said Jim.

He was very serious. It was the first time she had seen him in that mood and she rather liked it.

'Only one more question. You don't know that he is in any way connected with a firm called Rata?'

And, when she confessed that she had never heard of such a firm, his seriousness was at an end.

'And that's the whole of the questionnaire, back page and everything!'

He leaned back to allow the burly waiter to place the dish on the table.

'*Sole bonne femme* is good for the tired business girl. Will you have wine, or just the Lord's good water?'

After this he became his old flippant self. He made no further allusion to her uncle; and if he talked a great deal about himself, it was interesting, for he talked shop, and Scotland Yard shop is the second most interesting in the world. He lived at his club.

'I'd better give you the telephone number in case you ever want me.' He scrawled the address on the back of the menu and tore off the corner.

'Why should I want you?'

'I don't know. I've just got a feeling that you might. I'm a hunch merchant – do you know what a hunch merchant is?'

She could guess.

'Premonitions are my long suit, telepathy my sixth sense, and I've got a hunch ... perhaps I'm wrong. I hope I am.'

Once or twice he had looked at his watch, a little furtively, she thought, yet it seemed that he was prepared to break any appointment he had made, for he lingered over his coffee until she brought a happy evening to an abrupt close by putting on her gloves. As they were driving back to her rooms:

'I haven't asked you very much about yourself. That is the kind of impertinence which really scares me,' he said, 'but I gather that you're unmarried – and unengaged?' he asked.

'I have no followers,' she said without embarrassment, 'and I hope that confession will offer no encouragement to the philandering constabulary!'

He chuckled for fully a minute.

'That's good,' he said at last. ' "Philandering constabulary" is taken into use for special occasions. You're the first woman—'

'Don't!' she warned him.

'—I've ever met with a real sense of humour,' he concluded. 'I'm sorry to disappoint you.'

'I wasn't disappointed. I expected something banal,' she

said. 'My house is the third on the left ... thank you.'

She got down without assistance and offered her hand, and as he looked past her towards the door of the house:

'The number is 163,' she said, 'but you needn't write unless you've something very policey to write about. Good night!'

Jim Carlton was smiling all the way to Whitehall Gardens and his sense of amusement still held when he followed the footman into Sir Joseph Layton's study.

The words 'Joseph Layton' are familiar to all who carry passports, for he was the Foreign Secretary, a man of slight figure and ascetic face; and possibly the most cartooned politician in Britain.

He looked up over his big horn-rimmed glasses as Jim came in.

'Sit down, Carlton.' He blotted the letter he had been writing, inserted it with punctilious care into an envelope, and addressed it with a flourish before he spoke.

'I've just come back from the House. Did you call before?'

'No, sir.'

'Humph!'

He settled himself more easily in his padded chair, put the tips of his fingers together, and again scrutinised the detective over his glasses.

'Well, what are the developments?' he asked, and added: 'I've seen the cables you sent me. Curious – very curious indeed. You intercepted them?'

'Some of them, sir,' said Jim. 'A great deal of the correspondence of the Rata Syndicate goes through other channels. But there's enough to show that Rata is there preparing for a big killing. I should imagine that every big broking house in the world has received similar instructions.'

Sir Joseph unlocked a drawer of his desk and, pulling it open, took out a number of sheets of paper fastened together by a big brass clip. He turned the leaves slowly.

'I suppose this one is typical,' he said.

It was a message addressed to Rata Syndicate, Wall Street:

Be ready to sell for 15 per cent. drop undermentioned securities.

Here followed a long list that covered two pages of writing, and against each stock was the number to be sold.

'Yes,' said Sir Joseph, stroking his little white moustache thoughtfully. 'Very peculiar, very remarkable! As you said in your letter, these are the very stocks which would be instantly affected by the threat of war. But who on earth are we going to fight? The International situation was never easier. The Moroccan question has been settled. You read my speech in the House last night?'

Jim nodded.

'Upon my word,' said Sir Joseph, 'I think I was very careful to avoid anything like unjustifiable optimism, but, searching the world from East to West, I can see no single cloud on the horizon.'

Jim Carlton reached out, took the papers and read them through carefully.

'I think,' said the Foreign Minister with a twinkle in his eye, 'you have at the back of your mind the vision of some diabolical conspiracy to embroil the world in war. Am I right? Secret agents, traffic in secret plans, cellar meetings with masked and highly-placed diplomats?'

'Nothing so romantic,' smiled Jim. 'No; I wasn't brought up in that school. I know how wars are made. They grow as storms grow – out of the mists that gather on marshlands and meadows. Label them "the rising clouds of national prejudice," and you've got a rough illustration.'

'Come now, Mr Carlton, who is your ideal conspirator? I'm sure I know. You think Harlow is behind Rata; and that he has some diabolical scheme for stirring up the nations?'

'I think Harlow is behind most of the big disturbances,' said Jim slowly. 'He's got too much money; can't you get some of it away from him?'

'We do our best,' said the Foreign Minister dryly; 'but

he's one of the few people in England who can look the sur-tax collector in the eye and never quail!'

Jim went back to Scotland Yard expecting to find Elk, but learned that that intelligent officer had left earlier in the evening for Devonshire. He was to meet Ingle on his release from prison and accompany him to town. And Inspector Elk's mission was certainly not on Aileen's behalf, nor had he any humanitarian idea of preparing the convict for news of the burglary.

The first idea (and this proved to be wrong) was that there was a reason and a mind behind this crime. Some-thing had been taken of such value as justified the risk. The sudden appearance of Harlow in the flat immediately after the crime had been committed had convinced Carlton that his visit was associated with the safe robbery. Harlow should have been at a City banquet – Jim had been trailing him all that day, and had known his destination. Indeed, his name had appeared in the morning newspapers as having been present at the dinner. And yet, within an hour of the accident on the Embankment, Harlow had turned up at Fotheringay Mansions, and had not deigned to offer an excuse for his absence from the dinner, although Jim was sure he knew that he had been trailed.

The early morning found Inspector Elk shivering on the wind-swept platform of Princetown. There were very few people in the waiting train at that hour; a workman or two on their way to an intermediate station, a commercial traveller who had been detained overnight and was probably looking forward to the comforts of Plymouth, comprised the list. It was within a minute of starting time, and he was beginning to think that he had wasted his time getting up so early, when he saw two men walk on to the platform. One was a warder, and the other a thin man in an ill-fitting blue suit. The warder disappeared into the booking-office and came back with a ticket, which he handed to the other.

'So long, Ingle!' said the officer, and held out his hand, which the ex-convict took grudgingly.

Ingle stepped into the carriage and was turning to shut the door when Elk followed him and the recognition was immediate. Into the keen eyes of Arthur Ingle came a look of deep suspicion.

'Hallo! What do you want?' he asked harshly.

'Why, bless my life, if it isn't Ingle!' said Elk with a gasp. 'Well, well, well! It doesn't seem five years ago—'

'What do you want?' asked Ingle again.

'Me? Nothing! I've been up to the prison making a few inquiries about a friend of one of those mocking birds, but you know what they are – it was love's labour lost, so to speak,' said Elk, lighting a cigar and offering the case to his companion.

Ingle took the brown cylinder, smelt it and, biting off the end savagely, accepted the light which the detective held for him. By this time the train was moving and they were free from any possibility of interruption.

'Let me see: I heard something about you the other day ... What was it?' Mr Elk held his forehead, a picture of perplexity. 'I've got it!' he said. 'There was a burglary at your flat.'

The cigar dropped from the man's hand.

'A burglary?' he said shrilly. 'What was stolen?'

'Somebody opened the safe in your locker room—'

Ingle sprang to his feet, his teeth bared, his eyes glaring.

'The safe!' He almost screamed the words. 'Opened the safe – damn them! They're not satisfied with sending me to five years of this hell, but they want to catch me again, do they ...?'

Elk let him rave on until, in his rage, the man's voice sank to a hoarse rattle of sound.

'I hope you didn't lose any money?'

'Money!' snarled the man. 'Do you think I'm the kind who puts money in a safe? You know what I lost!' He pointed an accusing finger at the detective. 'You fellows did it! So that's why you're here, eh? A prison gate arrest, is it?'

'My dear, good man!' Elk was pained. 'I don't know what you're talking about! You're no more under arrest than I am. You could walk out of that door as free as the air, if the train wasn't moving.'

And then he asked:

'What did they pinch?'

It was a long time before the man recovered himself.

'If you don't know I'm not going to tell you,' he said. 'Some day—' He ground his teeth and in his eyes glared the fires of fanaticism. 'You, and the like of you, call me a thief!' His voice rose again as he talked rapidly. 'You branded me and put me into prison – segregated me from my kind . . . a pariah, a leper! For what? For skimming off a little of the stolen cream! For taking a little of the money wrested from sweating bodies and breaking hearts! It was mine - mine!' He struck his chest with a bony fist, his eyes blazing. 'The money belonged to me – to my fellows, to those men there!' He pointed back to where, beyond the brow of a rise, lay the grim prison building. 'I took it from those fat and greasy men and I'm glad of it! One jewel less for their horrible women; one motor-car fewer for their slaves to clean!'

'Great idea,' murmured Elk sympathetically.

'You! What are you? The lackey of a class,' sneered Ingle. 'The hired torturer - the prison-feeder!'

'Quite right,' murmured Elk, listening with closed eyes.

'If they found those papers they've something to think about - do you hear? - something to spoil their night's sleep! And if there is sedition in them I'm willing to go back to Princetown.'

Elk opened his eyes quickly.

'Oh, was that what it was?' he asked, disappointed. 'Revolution stuff?'

The man nodded curtly.

'I thought it was something worth while!' said Elk, annoyed. 'Silly idea though, isn't it, Ingle?'

'To you, yes. To me, no,' snapped the other. 'I hate

England! I hate the English! I hate all middle-class people, the smirking self-satisfied swine! I hated them when I was a starving actor and they sat in their stalls with a sneer on their overfed faces. . . .' He choked.

'There's a lot to be said for fat people,' mused Elk. 'Now take Harlow – though you wouldn't call him a fat man.'

'Harlow!' scoffed the other. 'Another of your moneyed gods!'

Evidently he remembered something, for he stopped suddenly.

'Moneyed gods—?' suggested Elk.

'I don't know.' The man shook his head. 'He may not be what he seems. In there' – he jerked his head backwards – 'they say he's crook to his back teeth! But he doesn't rob the poor. He takes it in large slabs from the fat men.'

'If that's so, I've nothing to say. He's on the side of law and order,' said Elk gently. 'A man who hands out police stations as Christmas presents can't be wholly bad!'

By the time the train pulled into Plymouth station, Detective-Inspector Elk was perfectly satisfied that there was nothing further to be learnt from the man. He went to the post office and sent a telegram to Jim which was short and expressive.

Revolution stuff. Nothing important.

He was on the same train that carried Mr Ingle to London, but he did not occupy the same compartment, except for half an hour after the train flashed through Bath, when he strolled into the carriage and sat down by the man's side; and apparently he was welcome, for Ingle started talking.

'Have you seen anything of my niece? Does she know about the burglary? I think you told me, but I was so angry that I can't remember.' And, when Elk had given him the fullest particulars: 'Harlow! Why did he come? He met Aileen at Dartmoor, you say?' He frowned and suddenly slapped his knee. 'I remember the fellow. He was sprawling in his car by the side of the road when we came back from the field that day. So that was Harlow! Does he know Aileen?' he asked suspiciously.

'They met at Dartmoor; that's all I know.'

Ingle gave one of his characteristic shrugs.

'I suppose he's running after her? She's a pretty sort of girl. With that type of man, money's no object. She's old enough to look after herself without my assistance.'

So this Utopian left Aileen Rivers to her fate.

7

HE HAD wired from Plymouth asking her to call at the flat that night, and she arrived just as he had finished a dinner he had cooked for himself.

'Yes, I've heard about the burglary,' he said, cutting short her question. 'They've got nothing that was worth a shilling to them, thank God! Why did you call in the police?'

And then he had a shock.

'Who else should I have called in – a doctor?' she asked.

It was the first time he had met her in a period of freedom. She had had her instructions to look after the flat, smuggled out of prison by a discharged convict; and their talks during the brief visiting hours had been mainly on business.

'What does one usually do when a burglary is discovered?' she asked. 'I sent for the police – of course I sent!'

He stared at her fiercely, but she did not flinch. It was his eyes which dropped first.

'I suppose it's all right,' he said, and then: 'You know Harlow, don't you?'

'I met him at Dartmoor, yes.'

'A friend of yours?'

'No more than you are,' she said; and he had his second shock.

'I'm not going to quarrel with you, and I don't see why you should want to be rude to me,' he snapped. 'You've been useful, but I've not been ungenerous. Harlow is a friend of yours—'

'He called here on the night of the burglary to offer me a job,' she replied, without any visible evidence of her rising anger. 'I met him at Princetown and he seemed to think that because of my relationship with you, I should find it rather difficult to get employment.'

He muttered something under his breath which she did not catch and it occurred to her that she had cowed this bullying little man, though she had had no such intention.

'I shall not want you any more.' He took out his pocket-book, opened it and extracted a banknote. 'This is in the nature of a bonus,' he said. 'I do not intend continuing your allowance.'

He expected her to refuse the money and he was not wrong.

'Is that all?' she asked. She did not attempt to take the note.

'That is all.'

With a nod she turned and walked to the door.

'The charwoman is coming tonight to clean up,' she said. 'You had better make arrangements for her to stay on – but I suppose you've already made your plans.'

Before he could reply, she was gone. He heard the street door slam after her, took up the money and put it back in his case; and he was without regret for, if the truth be told, Mr Arthur Ingle, despite the largeness of his political views, was exceedingly mean.

There was a great deal for him to do: old boxes to open and sort, papers and memoranda to retrieve from strange hiding-places. The seat of the big settee on which Aileen had sat so often waiting for the cleaner to finish her work, opened like a lid and here he had documents and, in a steel box, passbooks that might not have come to light even if the police had been aware of the flat at the time of his arrest, and had made their usual search.

Ingle was a man of wide political activities. No party man in the sense that he found a party to match his own views; rather, he was one of those violent and compelling thinkers who are unconsciously the nucleus of a movement. His grudge against the world was a sincere one. He saw injustice in the simplest consequences of cause and effect. His opinions had not made him a thief; they had merely justified him in his disregard for the law and his obligation to society. Imprisonment had made him neither better nor worse, had merely confirmed him in certain theories. Inconsistently, he loathed his prison associates, men who had been unsupported by his high motives in their felonies. The company of them was contamination. He hated the chaplain; and only one inmate of that terrible place touched what in him still remained tender. That was the old, blind horse who had his stable in the prison, and whose sight seemed to have been destroyed by Providence that he might not witness the degradation of the superior mammals that tramped the exercise ring, or went trudging and shuffling up the hill and through the gates.

He was the one man in the prison who was thankful when the cell door closed on him and the key turned in the lock. The foulness of these old lags, their talk, their boasts, the horrible things that may not be written about ... he could not think back without feeling physically sick. In truth he would not have stretched out his hand if, by so doing, he could have opened those cell doors and released to the world the social sweepings whom it was his professed mission to salve.

His work finished, he lit a cigarette, fitted it carefully into an amber holder and, adjusting the cushions, lay down on the settee and smoked and thought till the telephone bell roused him and he got up.

The voice that spoke to him was quite unfamiliar.

'Is that Mr Ingle?'

53

'Yes,' he said shortly.

'Will you make a sacrifice of your principles?' was the astonishing request, and the man smiled sourly.

'What I have left, yes. What do you wish?'

It might be an old friend in need of money, in which case the conversation would be short. For Arthur Ingle had no foolish ideas about charity.

'Could you meet me tonight on the sidewalk immediately opposite Horse Guards Parade?'

'In the park, you mean?' asked Ingle, astonished. 'Who are you? I'll tell you before you go any further that I'm not inclined to go out of my way to meet strangers. I'm a pretty tired man tonight.'

'My name is—' a pause – 'Harlow.'

Involuntarily, Ingle uttered an exclamation.

'Stratford Harlow?' he asked incredulously.

'Yes, Stratford Harlow.'

There was a long pause before Arthur Ingle spoke.

'It's rather an extraordinary request, but I realise that it isn't an idle one. How do I know you're Harlow?'

'Call me up in ten minutes at my house and ask for me,' said the voice. 'Will you come?'

Again Mr Ingle hesitated.

'Yes, I'll come,' he said. 'At what time?'

'At ten o'clock exactly. I won't keep you hanging about this cold night. You can get into my car and we'll drive somewhere.'

Ingle hung up the telephone a little bewildered. He was a cautious man and after ten minutes had expired he put through the number he discovered in the phone directory, and the same voice answered him.

'Are you satisfied?'

'Yes, I'll be there – ten o'clock,' he said.

He had two hours to wait. The charwoman did not arrive till nine. He gave her instructions, made arrangements for the following day; and went back to the dining-room to think out the extraordinary request which Stratford Harlow had made of him. And the more he thought, the less inclined he was to keep the appointment. At last he turned to his writing table, took out a sheet of paper and scrawled a note.

DEAR MR HARLOW,

I am afraid I must disappoint you. I am in such a position, being an ex-convict, that I cannot afford to take the slightest risk. I will tell you frankly that what I have in my mind is that this may be a frame-up organised by my friends the police, and I think that it would be, to say the least, foolish on my part to go any farther until I know your requirements, or at least have written proof that you have approached me.

Yours sincerely,
ARTHUR INGLE.

He put the letter in an envelope, addressed it, and marked in the corner in bold letters 'By hand. Urgent.' Even now he was not satisfied. He went to the telephone to call a district messenger, but he did not lift the receiver. His curiosity was piqued. He felt he must know, with the least possible delay, just why Stratford Harlow had summoned Arthur Ingle, late of Dartmoor convict establishment. And why should the meeting be secret? A man of Harlow's standing would not lose caste, even if he sent for him to go to his house. He came to a sudden resolve, pitched the letter on to the table, went into his bedroom and changed into a dark suit.

By the time he had climbed into his overcoat he was satisfied that he was taking the wisest course. The charwoman was in the kitchen and he opened the door to pass his last admonition. She was on her knees, scrubbing-brush in hand, and he looked down into a long, weak face over which strayed lank wisps of grey-black hair.

'I'm going out. You needn't wait. Finish your work and be here in the morning before eight,' he barked and slammed the door on this inconsiderable member of the proletariat and went down the stairs in a spirit of adventure that made him feel almost young.

As the Horse Guards clock was chiming the three-quarters he came into Birdcage Walk and turned along the lonely

55

footpath that runs parallel with the Horse Guards and flanks the broad parade ground. There was no hurry; he fell into a gentle stroll, fast enough to keep him warm and to avoid any suspicion of loitering within the meaning of the act.

It could not be a frame-up, he had decided. A man of Harlow's character would hardly lend himself to such a plot; and in his heart of hearts, for all his bitter gibes at the police, he did not believe seriously in the prison legend of innocent men being trapped by cunning police plots.

He looked at his watch under a street standard; it was five minutes to ten, and he strolled back the way he had come, and stopped immediately in a line with the gates that closed the arch of the Horse Guards. As he did so a car came noiselessly along the sidewalk from the direction of Westminster. It stopped in front of him and the door opened.

'Will you come in, Mr Ingle?' said a low voice; and without a word he stepped inside, pulling the door close after him and sank down on a soft seat by the side of a man who, he at once recognised, was that Splendid Harlow, whose name, even in Dartmoor, symbolised wealth beyond dreams.

The car, gathering speed, turned into the Mall, swung round towards Buckingham Palace and across the Corner into Hyde Park. It slackened speed now, and Stratford Harlow began to talk . . .

For an hour the car moved at a leisurely pace round the Circle. Sleet was falling. Ingle listened like a man in a dream to the amazing proposition which his companion advanced.

He, at any rate, sat in comfort. Inspector Jim Carlton, following in an aged convertible was chilled and wet, and the highly sensitive microphone which he had placed in Harlow's car failed to transmit the talk it was so vital he should hear.

Arthur Ingle arrived home at his flat soon after eleven. The cleaner had gone and he was glad; dull clod and unimaginative as she was she yet might have read and interpreted the light that shone in his eyes or have sensed the exultation of his heart.

Brewing himself some coffee, he sat down at his desk and began to make notes. Once he rose and, entering his bed-room, turned on the light above his dressing-table and stared at himself for five minutes in the glass. The scrutiny seemed to afford him a certain amount of satisfaction, for he smiled and returned to his notemaking.

That smile did not leave his lips; and once he laughed out loud. Evidently something had happened that afforded him the most exquisite happiness.

8

Could you please come and see me in the lunch hour?—A.R.

JIM CARLTON looked at the 'A.R.' blankly before he placed 'A' as indicating Aileen – he was under the impres-sion that she spelt her name with an 'E'. It had been delivered at Scotland Yard by a messenger half an hour before he arrived. Literally he was waiting on the mat when the girl came out; and she seemed very glad to see him.

'You will probably be very angry that I've sent for you about such a little thing,' she said, 'and you're so busy—'

'I won't tell you how I feel about it,' he interrupted, 'or you'll think I'm not sincere.'

'You see, you are the only policeman I know and I don't know you very well, but I thought you wouldn't mind. Mrs Gibbins has disappeared; she didn't go home last night nor the night before.'

'I'm thrilled,' he said. 'And her husband fears the worst?'

'She hasn't a husband; she's a widow. Her landlady came in to see me this morning. She's dreadfully upset.'

'But who's Mrs Gibbins?'

'Mrs Gibbins is the charwoman at Uncle's flat. Rather a wretched-looking lady with untidy hair. I'm rather worried about it because she's a woman without friends. I called up my Uncle's flat this morning and he was almost polite, and told me that she didn't arrive yesterday morning and she hasn't been there today.'

'She may have met with an accident,' was his natural suggestion.

'I've telephoned to the big hospitals, but nothing has been heard of her. I want you to tell me what I can do next. It's such a little matter that I'll listen meekly to any rude comment you care to think up!'

He was not interested in Mrs Gibbins; the case of a lonely woman who disappears as from the face of the earth was so common a phenomenon in the life of any great city that he could hardly work up enthusiasm for the search. But Aileen was so concerned that he would have been a brute to have treated her request lightly; and after lunch, the day being his own, he went to Stanmore Rents in Lambeth, a little riverside slum and made a few inquiries at first hand.

Mrs Gibbins had lived there, the slatternly landlady told him, for five years. She was a good, sober, honest woman, never went out, had no friends, and subsisted on what she earned and a pound a week which was paid to her quarterly by some distant relation. In fact, she was due to receive the money on the following Monday. Her chief virtue was that she paid her rent every Monday morning and gave no trouble.

'Do you mind if I search her room?'

The landlady wished that and showed him the way; it gave her a nice feeling of authority to be present during the operation.

Jim was shown into a small back room, scrupulously clean, with a bed and a sort of home-made hanging cupboard that had been fixed in one corner and was shrouded by a cheap curtain. Here was the meagre wardrobe of the missing char-woman: a skirt or two, a light summer coat that had seen its brightest days, and a best hat. He tried the chest of drawers and found one drawer locked. This he opened with the first key on his own bunch, to the awe and admiration of the landlady. Here was proof of the woman's affluence – a post office bank-book showing £87 to her credit, four new £1 Treasury notes, and a threadbare bag with a broken catch. Inside this were one or two proofs of the vanity of the eternal feminine – a greasy powder-puff, a cheap trinket or two, and between lining and outer cover a folded paper of some sort. It had not got there by accident, he saw, when he carried the bag to the light, for it was carefully sewn into the lining. He took out his pocket knife and, picking the stitches, extracted what he thought was one sheet of paper, lightly folded. When he opened the paper out he found there were two sheets.

The landlady ducked her head sideways in an effort to catch a glimpse of the writing, but Jim was aware of this manoeuvre.

'Do you mind going downstairs,' he asked politely, 'and seeing if you can find in your ash-can—'

'Dustbin,' corrected the lady.

'Whatever it is, the envelope of any letter addressed to Mrs Gibbins?'

By the time she returned from her profitless task the papers had disappeared, and Jim Carlton was sitting on the narrow window ledge, a cigar between his teeth and he was examining the threadbare carpet with such intentness that the landlady was certain that he had discovered some blood-stains.

'Eh?' He woke from his dream with a start. 'You can't find it? I'm sorry. What was it I asked you to get? Oh, yes, an envelope. Thank you. I found it in the bag.'

He relocked the drawer, and with another glance round the apartment came down the treacherous stairs.

'You don't think she's drownded herself, sir?' asked the landlady tremulously.

'No. Why? Did she ever threaten to commit suicide?'

'She's been pretty miserable for some time, poor dear!' The woman wiped a tear from her cheek, and the fascinated Jim observed that the spot where the apron had been rubbed was perceptibly cleaner.

'No, I don't think she has – committed suicide,' he said.

'She may turn up. If she does, will you send me a telegram?'

He scribbled his name and address on a blank that he found in his pocket and gave her the money for its dispatch.

'I know there's something wrong,' insisted the tearful lady. 'Foul play or something. She bought some stuff to make up into a dress; I've got it in my kitchen – it only came the night before last.'

She showed him the package, which was unopened.

'My niece was coming in yesterday morning to show her how to cut it out,' continued the woman, 'but, of course, Mrs Gibbins didn't come home, and my niece lives over in Peckham, and it's a long drag here—'

'Yes. I suppose so,' said Jim absently.

He walked down the noisome street, got into the car that was waiting at the end, and went slowly back across Westminster Bridge to his room.

Elk was not in and, even if he had been, Jim was not in the mood for consultation. He spread out on the table the papers he had taken from Mrs Gibbins's bag and read them carefully, jotted down a few particulars and, refolding them, put them in his pocket-book. He passed the next hour dictating letters to the last people in the world one would have imagined would be interested in the disappearance of a charwoman.

Aileen did not expect to see him again that day and was surprised, almost pleasurably, when he walked into the outer office and sent in his name. She was on the point of leaving and the office boy, impatient to be gone, misinterpreted the colour that came to her cheeks.

'You'll be getting me a very bad name, Mr Carlton,' she said as they went into the street together.

'Did I tell you that my front name was Jim, or James, as the case may be?' he asked. 'Shall we try something more snappy in the restaurant line? I know a place in Soho—'

'No, I think I'll go home now.'

'I wanted to talk to you about our Mrs Gibbins,' he said flippantly, though he was not feeling at all flippant. 'And I have told our people that I can be found there if I am wanted.'

'Have you had any news?' she asked; and he guessed by her penitent tone that she had altogether forgotten the existence of the charwoman. At any rate she did not demur when he handed her into the car and she accepted his restaurant, dingy though it was, without protest.

They were passing from the street when Jim heard his name called and, looking round, saw a headquarters man.

'Came through just after you left, sir.'

Jim read the hastily-written phone message.

'I'll be back in an hour,' he said, and followed the girl who was waiting for him in the vestibule.

When they were seated:

'I want to ask you: was Mrs Gibbins in the flat that night your uncle's safe was burgled?'

She considered.

'No, she wasn't there; at least, she oughtn't to have been there. She came later, you remember. I opened the door to her.'

'Oh!' he said, and she smiled.

'What does "Oh!" mean?' And then quickly: 'You don't think she was the burglar, do you?'

'No, I don't think that,' he said; his tone was very grave – she wondered why. 'Tell me something about her; was she well educated?'

Aileen shook her head.

'No, she was rather illiterate. I've had many of her notes, and they were scarcely decipherable. The spelling was – well, very original.'

'Oh!' he said again, and she could have boxed his ears.

'Well, that's that!' he said at last. 'I don't think that even your uncle, with his well-known passion for humanity, will so much as shed a silent tear. She was just nothing, nobody – a wisp of straw caught up in the wind and deposited God knows where! Stale fruit under the dustman's broom. Horrible, isn't it? Think of it! All the theatres will soon be crowded and people will be screaming with laughter at the antics and clowning of the comedians! There will be a State ball at the Palace and tonight happy men and women will be dancing on a hundred floors. Who cares about Mrs Gibbins?'

He was very serious, and a minute before he had been almost gay.

'The passing of a friendless woman is a small thing.' He rubbed his nose irritably. 'And now it is a big thing!' he said, raising a warning finger and looking at her. 'Mrs Gibbins is stirring the minds of eighteen thousand London policemen, who if need be would have the support of the whole Brigade of Guards and every one of these dancers, diners and theatregoers would move with one accord and not rest day or night till they found the man who struck her down and dropped her poor, wasted body in the waters of the Regent's Canal!'

She half rose, but he motioned her down.

'I've spoilt your dinner and I've spoilt my own, too,' he said.

'Dead?' she whispered.

He nodded.

'Murdered?'

'Yes ... I think so. They took her out of the canal a few minutes before I left the office, and there were marks to show that she'd been bludgeoned. I had the news just before I came in. What was she doing near the Edgware Road – in Regent's Park, let us say? Give her two days to drift as far.'

The waiter came and stood at his elbow in an attitude of expectancy. The girl shook her head.

'I can't eat.'

'Omelettes,' said Jim. 'That isn't eating; it's just nourishment.'

Arthur Ingle had the discomfort of a police visitation, but he knew nothing of Mrs Gibbins, knew much less indeed than his niece.

'I have seen the woman, but I shouldn't recognise her.'

62

This accorded with the information already in their possession and the two detectives who called had a whisky-and-soda with him and departed.

The landlady of the Rents could say no more than she had said on the previous afternoon to Sub-Inspector Carlton.

Jim went down himself to see this worthy soul; and he had a particular reason, because on that morning, 'regular as clockwork,' came the envelope which contained Mrs Gibbins's quarterly allowance; and that lady was rather in a fluster, because the letter had not arrived.

'No, sir, it was never registered, that's why I feel so awkward about it. People might think ... but you can ask the postman yourself, sir.'

'I've asked him,' smiled Jim. 'Tell me, where were those letters posted? You must have seen the date-stamp at some time or other.'

But she swore she hadn't; she was not inquisitive, indeed regarded inquisitiveness as one of the vices which had come into existence with reading newspapers. She did not explain the connection between the popular press and the inquiring mind, though it was there plain to be seen.

The local police inspector had cleared the wardrobe and drawers of all portable articles, including the bag.

'I told him you found a paper in the bag, but he couldn't see it, sir, though he searched high and low for it.'

'There wasn't a paper to find,' said Jim untruthfully.

His position was a delicate one. He had withdrawn important evidence from what might perhaps be a very serious case. There was only one course to take and this he followed. Returning to Scotland Yard, he requested an interview with the Commissioners, explained what he had done, told them frankly his suspicions and asked for the suppression of the evidence he held. The consultation was postponed for the attendance of a representative of the Public Prosecutor, but in the end he had his way, and when the inquest was held on Annie Maud Gibbins the jury returned an open verdict, which meant that they were content with the statement that the deceased woman had been 'found dead', and expressed no opinion as to how she met her fate – a laudable verdict, since no member of the jury, not even the coroner, nor the doctors who testified with so many reservations, had the slightest idea how the life of Mrs Gibbins, the charlady, had gone out.

9

AILEEN RIVERS was annoyed, and since the object of her annoyance lived in the same room, and to use a vulgar idiom, under the same hat as herself, a highly unsatisfactory state of affairs was produced. She was annoyed because she had not seen Mr James Carlton for a week. But she was furious with herself that she was annoyed at all. Mr Stebbings, that stout lawyer, had reached an age when he was no longer susceptible to atmosphere, yet even he was conscious that his favourite employee had departed in some degree from the normal. He asked her if she was not well; and suggested that she should take a week off and go to Margate. The suggestion of Margate was purely mechanical; he invariably prescribed Margate for all disorders of body and mind, having been once in the remote past cured of the whooping cough in that delightful town. It was not Margate weather, and Aileen was not Margate-minded.

'I remember' – Mr Stebbings unfolded several of his heavy chins to gaze meditatively at the ceiling – 'many years ago suggesting to Miss Mercy Harlow – ahem!—'

It occurred to him that the girl would not know Miss Mercy Harlow and that the name would be without significance; for the great heights to which the living Harlow had risen were outside his comprehension.

'You used to act for the Harlows once, didn't you, Mr Stebbings?'

'Yes,' said Mr Stebbings carefully. 'It was – er – a great responsibility. I was not sorry when young Mr Stratford went elsewhere.'

He said no more than this, which was quite a lot for Mr Stebbings, but by one of those coincidences which are a daily feature of life she came again into contact with the Harlow family.

Mr Stebbings was dealing with a probate case. A will had been propounded in the court, and was being opposed by a distant relative of the legator. The question turned on whether, in the spring of a certain year the legator had advanced certain money to one of the numerous beneficiaries under the will with the object of taking him out of the country. Aileen was sent to inspect the cash book, since it was alleged the money had been paid through the lawyers. She found the entry without a great deal of difficulty, and, running down the index to discover if she had missed any further reference, her finger stopped at the words:

Harlow – Mercy Mildred.
Harlow – Stratford Selwyn Mortimer.

She would not have been human if she had not turned up the pages. For a quarter of an hour she pored over the accounts of the dead and gone Miss Mercy, that stern and eccentric woman, and then she saw an item 'To L. Edwins, £125.' An entry occurred four months later: 'To L. Edwins, £183 17s. 4d.' She knew of Mrs Edwins, and had seen a copy of Miss Mercy Harlow's will – she had looked it up after the Dartmoor meeting, being momentarily interested in the millionaire.

She turned to Stratford's account, which was a very small one. Evidently, Mr Harlow made no payments through his lawyers. If an opportunity had occurred she would have asked Mr Stebbings for further information about the family, though she was fairly sure that such a request would have produced no satisfactory result.

Deprived of this interest, Aileen was thrown back upon

the dominating occupation of life – her amazement and disapproval of Aileen Rivers in relation to Mr James Carlton. He knew her address: she had particularly told him the number. Equally true it was that she had asked him only to write on official business. By some miracle she had not been called to give evidence at the inquest and she might, and did, trace his influence here. But even that could not be set against a week's neglect.

'Ridiculous' (said the saner part of her, in tones of reprobation). 'You hardly know the man! Just because he's been civil to you and has taken you out to dinner twice (and they were both more or less business occasions), you're expecting him to behave as though he were engaged to you!'

The unregenerate Aileen Rivers merely tossed her head at this and was unashamed.

She could, of course, have written to him: there was excuse enough; and she actually did begin a letter, until the scandalous character of her behaviour grew apparent even to Aileen II.

Saturday passed and Sunday; she stayed at home both days in case—

He called on Sunday night, when she had given up – well, if not hope, at any rate expectation.

'I've been down to the country,' he said.

She interviewed him in the sitting room which her landlady set aside for formal calls.

'Couldn't you come out somewhere? Have you dined?'

She had dined.

'Come along and walk; it's rather a nice night. We can have coffee somewhere.'

Her duty was to tell him that he was taking much for granted, but she didn't. She went upstairs, got her coat and in the shortest space of time was walking with him through Bloomsbury Square.

'I'm rather worried about you,' he said.

'Are you?' Her surprise was genuine.

'Yes, I am a little. Didn't you tell me once that Mrs Gibbins used to confide her troubles to you?'

There was a note of anxiety in his voice.

'She was rather confidential at times.'

'Did she ever tell you anything about her past?'

'Oh, no,' said Aileen quickly. 'It was mostly about her mother, who died about four years ago.'

'Did she ever tell you her Christian name – her mother's, I mean?'

'Louisa,' answered the girl promptly. 'You're awfully mysterious, Mr James Carlton. What has this to do with poor Mrs Gibbins?'

'Nothing, except that her name was Annie Maud, and the letters containing the money, which came to her quarterly, were addressed to "Louisa," 14 Kennet Road, Birmingham, and readdressed by the postal authorities. A letter came this morning.'

'Poor soul!' said the girl softly.

'Yes.'

It was surprising how well she understood him, remembering the shortness of their acquaintance. She knew, for example, when he was thinking of something else – his voice rose half a tone.

'Isn't that strange? Do you remember my telling you of the eighteen thousand policemen and the Brigade of Guards, and the whole congregation of the blessed? And now they are all agitated because Mrs Gibbins's mother was named Louisa! That discovery – I shouldn't have asked you, because I knew it already – proved two things: first, that Mrs Gibbins committed a crime some fifteen years ago, and secondly, that this is the second time she's been dead!'

He suddenly relaxed and laughed softly.

'Don't tell me,' he warned her. 'I know just the fictional detective whom I am imitating! The whole thing is rather complicated. Did I say coffee or dinner?'

'You said coffee,' she said.

The popular restaurant into which they went was just a

little overcrowded and after being served they lost no time in making their escape.

They were passing along Coventry Street when a big car rolled slowly past. The man who was driving was in evening dress ... they saw the sheen of his diamond studs, the red tip of his cigar.

'Nobody on earth but the Splendid Harlow could so scintillate,' said Jim. 'What does he do in this part of the world at such an hour?'

The car turned to the right through Leicester Square and passed down Orange Street at a pace which was strangely majestic. It was as though it formed part of and led a magnificent procession. The same thought occurred to both of them.

'He should really travel with a band!'

'I was thinking that, too,' laughed the girl. 'He frightened me terribly the night he came to the flat. I mean, when I opened the door to him. And I'm not easily scared. He looked so big and powerful and ruthless that my soul cowered before him!'

They passed up deserted Long Acre; it was too early for the market carts to have assembled, and the street was a wilderness. Suddenly the girl found her hand held loosely in Jim Carlton's. He was swinging it to and fro. The severer side of Miss Aileen Rivers closed its eyes and pretended not to see.

'I've got a very friendly feeling for you,' said Jim huskily. 'I don't know why, but I just have. And if you talk about the philandering constabulary, I will never forgive you.'

Three men had suddenly debouched from a side street; they were talking noisily and violently and were moving slowly towards them. Jim looked round: the only man in sight was walking in the opposite direction, having passed them a minute or so before.

'I think we'll cross the road,' he said. He took her arm, and, quickening his step, led her to the opposite sidewalk.

The quarrelling three turned back and Jim stopped.

'I want you to run back to the other end of Long Acre and fetch a policeman,' he said in a low voice. 'Will you do this for me? Run!'

Obediently she turned and fled, and as she did so one of the three came lurching towards him.

'What's the idea?' he said loudly. 'Can't we have an argument without you butting in?'

'Stay where you are, Donovan,' said Jim. 'I know you and I know just what you're after.'

'Get him,' said somebody angrily, and Jim Carlton whipped out the twelve inch length of jambok that he carried in his pocket and struck at the nearest man. As the flexible hide reached its billet the man dropped like one shot. In another second his two companions had sprung at the detective; and he knew that he was fighting, if not for his life, at any rate to save himself from an injury which would incapacitate him for months.

Again the jambok reached home; a second man reeled. And then a taxicab came flying down Long Acre with a policeman on each footboard. . . .

'No, not Bow Street,' said Jim, 'take them to Cannon Row.'

Aileen was in the taxicab, a most unheroic woman, on the verge of tears.

'I guessed what they were after,' said Jim, as they were driving home. 'It is one of the oldest tricks in the world, that rehearsed street fight.'

'But why? Why did they do it? Were they old enemies of yours?' she asked, bewildered.

'One,' he said. 'Donovan.' He carefully avoided her second question.

The presence of Mr Harlow in his lordly car was no accident. The car which passed down Orange Street was ostensibly carrying him to Vira's Club, but there was a short cut which brought him through St Martin's Lane to the end of Long Acre before the two walkers could possibly reach there. What was more important was that it was very clear to Jim that he and the girl were under observation, and had been followed that night from the moment he left the club where he lived, until the attack was delivered.

The reason for the hold-up was not difficult to understand, even supposing he ruled out the very remote possibility that it was associated with Mrs Gibbins's death. And that he must exclude, unless he gave Mr Harlow credit for supernatural powers.

He saw the girl to her boarding house and went back to Scotland Yard, to find a telegram awaiting him. It was from the detective force of Birmingham, and ran:

> Your inquiry 793 Mrs Louisa Gibbins, deceased. Letter which came to her regularly every quarter, and which was subsequently readdressed to Mrs Gibbins, of Stanmore Rents, Lambeth, invariably had Norwood postmark. This fact verified by lodger of late Mrs Gibbins of this town. Annie Maud Gibbins's real name, Smith. She married William Smith, a platelayer on Midland Railway. Further details follow, Hooge. Ends.

A great deal of this information was not new to Jim Carlton. But the Norwood postmark was invaluable, for in that suburb of London lived Mr Ellenbury. Further details he would not need.

But before that clue could be followed, Jim Carlton's attention was wholly occupied by the strange behaviour of Arthur Ingle, who suddenly turned recluse, declined all communication with the outside world and, locking himself in his flat, gave himself to the study of cinematography.

10

IN THE days which followed Jim Carlton was a busy man, and only once during the week did he find time to see Aileen, and then she related one of the minor troubles of life. A new boarder had come to the establishment where she lived, an athletic young man who occupied the room immediately beneath hers and whose apparent admiration took the form of following her to her work every morning at a respectful distance.

'I wouldn't mind that, but he makes a point of being in the neighbourhood of the office when I come out for lunch, and when I go home at nights.'

'Has he spoken to you?' asked Jim, interested.

'Oh, no, he's been most correct; he doesn't even speak at meals.'

'Bear with him,' said Jim, a twinkle in his eye. 'It is one of the penalties attached to the moderately good-looking.'

Jim interviewed the girl's new admirer.

'As a shadow you're a little on the heavy side, Brown,' he said. 'You should have found a way of watching her without her knowing.'

'I'm very sorry, sir,' said Detective Brown, and thereafter his espionage was less oppressive.

It was remarkable that in none of the excursions which Jim Carlton made from day to day did he once see Arthur Ingle. Deliberately he called at those restaurants and places of resort which in the old days were favoured by the man. It would not be a sense of shame or an unwillingness to meet old friends and associates of a more law-abiding life, that would keep him away. If anything, he was proud of his accomplishments, for by his fantastic twist of reasoning he had come to regard himself as a public benefactor. Nobody had seen him; even the comrades whom it was his joy to address in frowsy Soho halls had not been honoured by speech or presence.

'It almost looks as if he had gone over to the capitalists,' said one.

'I didn't notice the flags were flying in Piccadilly,' said Jim.

One night it happened that he found himself walking along the street at the back of Fotheringay Mansions and, looking up, noticed a bright light burning behind the green blind in an upper room. Mr Ingle's apartment was very easily located. There was a narrow parapet to identify the height; the lumber room where the light showed was four windows from the fire escape.

Elk was with him, and to that unenthusiastic man he confided his intentions.

'He'll start a squeal about police persecution,' suggested Elk.

Undeterred, Jim went up in the elevator, though the man in charge discouraged him.

'I don't think Mr Jackson is at home,' he said. 'A gentleman called an hour ago and knocked twice but could get no answer.'

'Maybe I can knock louder,' suggested Jim.

But ring and knock as he did, he had no answer. Yet, as he listened at the letterbox aperture, to make certain that the bell was ringing, he could have sworn he heard a stealthy footstep inside. Why was Ingle hiding?

There was, of course, the possibility that the man was engaged in some new piece of roguery. But from his experience of swindlers, Jim Carlton knew that they were never furtive when they were planning a coup.

The landing was deserted and he could wait without attracting to himself the suspicion of the lift man. Again he stooped and listened; and now he heard a sound which puzzled him – a rapid whirring. He had heard that noise before somewhere, and yet he could not locate or diagnose the sound. It came very faintly as through a closed door. ...

He saw the ascending light of the elevator and walked to the gate. Tha car passed to the next floor to discharge its passenger, and then came down to his level.

'Couldn't make him hear, I suppose, sir?' asked the elevator man, with the satisfaction of one whose dire prophecy has been realised. 'He won't see anybody these days. Why, he doesn't even come out for his meals.'

'He has a servant, hasn't he?'

'Not now,' said the lift-man gloomily, as they sank slowly

down the well. 'Used to have, but she—' He told the story of Mrs Gibbins. 'Now he gets his food and stuff delivered. I think Mr Jackson is going in for something unusual,' he added as they reached the ground floor and he pulled back the gates.

'What do you mean by "something unusual"?'

The man scratched his head.

'I don't know exactly. About four days ago a man came here with a long black box – the sort of thing that they use for carrying films—'

Films!

Now Jim Carlton understood. This was the sound he had heard: the whirr of a cine projector!

'He took it up and left it. I asked him if Mr Jackson was taking on film work, but he said nothing – the man who brought it, I mean. Of course, if I knew for certain that he had any celluloid stored on the premises, I'd have to report it. Fire risk. ...'

Jim listened without hearing. He was dumbfounded by the discovery. Every man has his secret weakness, but though he had credited Mr Arthur Ingle with many peculiarities, he had never suspected him of a passion for the cinema.

Elk was waiting outside, the stub of a cigar between his teeth, a large unfurled umbrella in his hand, and in a few words Jim told him what he had learnt.

'Pitchers!' said Elk, shaking his head. 'Never thought he would lower himself to that! Queer thing how these crooks sort of run to weakness one way or the other. I knew a man, the cleverest safe-breaker in Europe, who'd risk a lagging to get a game of ping-pong! There was another fellow named Moses who had the finest long-firm business in England—'

'Let us go round and look at the back of the house again,' Jim interrupted the reminiscences ruthlessly.

The bright light was showing again, clear through the dark green blinds, even as he looked it was extinguished, but when his eyes became accustomed to the darkness he could

73

see the reflected glow of another light. It was in this room, then, that Mr Ingle was engaged in his new hobby.

Jim looked naturally at the fire-escape. There was a wall to be scaled, or easier perhaps, a door into the courtyard of the building might be opened with one of his keys. But the door needed no forcing; it was unlocked and gave easy entry to a stone-paved yard, whence a flight of iron stairs led up to the roof. An iron bar was fastened across the rails at the bottom, for what purpose was not clear, since it was possible to get either over or beneath it.

'Maybe it's to keep it airtight,' suggested Elk, 'or to trip up the fellers that are not burnt to death. Going up?'

Jim nodded, and Inspector Elk followed him from landing to landing until they came level with the floor on which Mr Ingle's flat was situated. Without a word, Jim Carlton swung himself over the rail and, balancing precariously upon the narrow ledge of stone, felt forward and gripped the nearest window-sill. Progress in front of the windows was an easy matter to one with his nerves: it was in the intervening spaces, where he had to depend for his life upon a fine sense of balance, that the danger lay. Elk watched him anxiously as he moved nearer and nearer to the window, flattening himself against the wall and edging forward inch by inch; in this perilous fashion, he came sidling to the window from behind which came the ceaseless rattle of the projector.

The moment he reached his objective Jim knew that his effort had been in vain. Behind blind and window he could see the small projector at work, was dazzled by the flicker of the light, and Arthur Ingle showed clearly in the glow thrown back from the invisible screen. He was staring at the picture which he was projecting, and the first thing the detective noticed was that Mr Ingle was in need of a barber, for his face was covered by a ragged white stubble and his grey hair was long and unkempt.

But what was the picture he was viewing so intently? Jim screwed his head round, but on the left-hand side of the window the blind ran flush with the sash. There was nothing to do but to make his way back and noiselessly he edged towards the fire ladder.

He had not gone more than halfway before he had a shock. He felt a stone yield beneath his feet, the edge broke off and fell into the courtyard below. It might be one rotten piece, he argued, but stepped more carefully. If the parapet gave under his weight while he was traversing a wall space, nothing could save him from death; but he did not allow his mind to dwell upon this aspect of the adventure.

He had reached the window nearest to the iron stairs and was feeling cautiously along with his feet when, without warning, the narrow parapet beneath him cracked. He managed to grip the wooden window; and in another second was hanging with his legs in space. He heard Elk's agitated whisper, saw the elderly detective thrust up the crook of his umbrella, but knew that this was beyond his reach.

There was only one hope; taking off his soft felt hat, he put his hand inside and drove straight at the glass of the window. The shock of the blow almost dislodged him, but clearing off the broken edge of glass, he took a firm grip of the window-sash and drew himself up. A second pane was broken in the same way and, reaching in, with some difficulty he turned the window catch and pushed up the sash. In another second he was in a room. He stopped to listen. The smashing of the glass had evidently not aroused the inmates and he passed out the news to the agitated Elk.

'I don't know whose flat it is,' he whispered. 'Meet me at the front of the building.'

Tiptoeing across the room, he felt for the light and turned it on. He was in a small bedroom, which had evidently not received any attention for a very considerable time, for dust lay thick upon the furniture and upon the folded blankets at the foot of the bed. Yet the room was handsomely furnished and in a style that harmonised with the general furnishings of Ingle's apartment. Evidently this was one of the rooms which he had not visited.

He opened the door carefully. The dining-hall was in

darkness; from the lumber-room came the ceaseless clickety-click of the projector.

Should he risk being discovered and satisfy his curiosity?

It was almost worth while. As he debated the point, the telephone rang noisily in the dining-room and he drew back, pulling the door close. He heard the snap as Ingle turned on the lights. ...

'Hullo! – yes, Jackson ... oh, is that you? Speaking from a call-box, I hope? Good! Yes, everything is OK . . . Yes, I've heard him – but only on the radio. I shall have to go to a meeting. He's a good speaker? Huh! So am I! A spell-binder – you can laugh! I've had four thousand people cheering for two minutes. Don't worry ... no, thanks, I have all the money I need.'

The receiver thudded down and presently the lights went out and the lumber-room door closed.

A spell-binder? Who was to be bound by the eloquence of Mr Arthur Ingle?

He waited until he heard the projector whirring again, and then, tiptoeing across the room, reached the passage. He was sorely tempted to take one look at the film show, but obviously he could only do this with the certainty that he would be seen, and Jim had all a detective's horror of a 'police persecution' charge.

He turned his flashlight on the table: there might be something there which would give him a clue. He saw a fat envelope bearing the name of the Cunard Company. This had not been opened, but he could guess its contents. Mr Ingle contemplated a visit to the United States – or Canada, perhaps.

The turning of the projector ceased. He passed quickly to the hall, opened the door and closed it quietly after him. The elevator was ascending as he went down, and he was spared an explanation of his surprising presence. He found the patient Elk flapping his hands to keep warm and puffing at the last few centimetres of his cigar.

Fortunately Jim's club was within a quarter of an hour's walk, and as they crossed the park Elk asked:

'You got into old man Ingle's flat, didn't you?'

'Looks like it.'

'What's thrillin' him?' asked Elk. 'I hate admittin' it, but the cinema's my favourite sleepin' place. Or was he runnin' through the cartoons?'

'I'd give a lot to know,' said Jim, and repeated the conversation he had overheard.

'Never know whether Arthur's red because he's wild, or wild because he's red,' mused Elk. 'He's a bit of a dilly – what's the word? – dilly-tanty, that's it. There's quite a lot of genuine Reds, but a whole lot of people who hang on in the hope that one of the comrades will break a jeweller's window so that they can get away with the doin's. Most people are Red if they only knew it. Take the feller that keeps beehives. He just waits for the old capitalist bee to pile up his honey reserves and then he comes down on his bank-roll. ...'

He philosophised thus all the way across the park.

'I am almost at the end of my theories – what is yours, Elk?'

'Beer,' said Elk absently, as they mounted the steps of the club.

'Looks like he's gettin' ready for a quick money stunt,' said Elk, as they made their way to the coffee-room. 'But, Lord, you can never follow the minds of people like Ingle! And he's an actor too – that makes him more skittish. As likely as not he's goin' to give lectures on "My Five Years of Hell" – they all do it.'

Jim shook his head helplessly.

'I don't know what to make of that film craze of his.'

'Decadence,' said Elk laconically. 'All these birds go wrong some way or another, I tell you.'

The waiter was hovering at their elbow.

'Beer,' said Elk emphatically.

It was a bitterly cold night, and in spite of the briskness

of their walk Jim had been glad to get into the comfort of his club. He had no intention of returning to Scotland Yard that night, and was in fact parting with Elk at the door that looks out upon Pall Mall when the club porter called him. There was an urgent message for him and, going into the booth, he spoke to one of the chief inspectors.

'I have been trying to get you all the evening,' said the officer. 'One of the park-keepers has found the place where he thinks Mrs Gibbins was thrown into the canal. I'm on the phone to him. He suggested you should meet him outside the Zoological Society's office.'

'Tell him that I'll come right along,' said Jim quickly, and returning to Elk, conveyed the gist of the message.

'Can't these amacher detectives find things in the Lord's bright sunlight?' asked Elk bitterly. 'Half-past nine and freezing like the devil: what a time to go snooping round canals!'

Yet he insisted upon going along with his companion.

'You might miss something,' he grumbled as the draughty taxi moved northward. 'You ain't got my power of observation and deduction. Anyway, I'll bet we're wasting our time. They'll show us the hole in the water where she went in most likely.'

'The canal is frozen,' smiled Jim. 'In fact, it's been frozen since the day after the body was found.'

Mr Elk growled something under his breath; whether it was an uncomplimentary reference to the weather or to the tardiness of park-keepers, Jim did not gather.

It was not a keeper but an inspector who was waiting for them outside the Zoological offices. The discovery had been made that afternoon, but the keeper had not reported the matter until late in the evening. The inspector took a seat in their taxi and under his direction they drove back some distance to the place where a bridge crosses the canal to Avenue Road. Here the Circle roadway is separated from the canal by a fifty-foot stretch of grassland and trees. This verge, in summer, affords a playing ground for children, and has, from their point of view, the attraction of dipping down in a steep slope to the banks of the canal, which, however, is separated from the park by a row of wooden palings, wired to form an unclimbable fence. The playground is reached from the road by a broad iron gate running parallel with the bridge, and this, explained the park inspector, was locked at nights.

'Occasionally somebody forgets,' he said, 'and I remember having it reported to me on the night after this woman's disappearance, that the gates were found open in the morning.'

He led the way cautiously down the steep declivity towards the fence which runs by the canal bank. Here is a rough path and along this they trudged over ground frozen hard.

'One of our keepers had to make an inspection of the fence this afternoon,' the officer went on, 'and we found that the palings had been wrenched from one of the supporting posts. Afterwards somebody must have put them up again and did the job so well that we have never noticed the break.'

They had now reached the spot, and a powerful light thrown along the fence revealed the extent of the damage. A wire strand and one of the palings had been broken, and the officer had only to push lightly at the fence to send it sagging drunkenly towards the canal. He put his foot upon it and with a creak it lay over so that he could have walked without any difficulty on to the canal bank.

'Our man thought that the damage had been done by boys, until he saw the hat.'

'Which hat?' asked Jim quickly.

'I left it here for you to see, exactly as he found it.'

The superintendent's light travelled along a bush, and presently focused upon a crushed brown object, which had been caught between two branches of the bush. Jim loosened the pitiable relic, a brown felt hat, stained and cut about the crown. It might easily, he saw, have been dragged off in a struggle, and against the autumnal colouring of the under-growth would have escaped notice.

'Here is another thing,' said the park officer. 'Do you see that? It was the first thing I looked for, but I have no doubt that you gentlemen will understand better than I what it signifies.'

It was the impress of a heel in the frozen ground. By its side a queer, flat footmark, criss-crossed with innumerable lines.

'Somebody who wore rubbers,' said Elk, going down on his knees. 'There has been a struggle here. Look at the side-ways thrust of that heel! And—'

'What is this?' asked Jim sharply.

His lamp was concentrated upon a tiny, frozen puddle, and Elk looked but could see nothing but its grey-white surface. Kneeling, Jim took out a knife from his pocket and began to scrape the ice; and now his companion saw what had attracted his attention: a piece of paper. It was an envelope which had been crushed into the mud. When he got the frozen object into the light it was frozen to the shape of the heel that had trodden upon it. Gently he scraped away the mud and ice until two lines were legible. The first was at the top left-hand corner and was heavily underlined.

By hand. Urgent.

Only one line of the address was legible, but the word 'Harlow' was very distinct.

They carried their find back to the superintendent's office and before his fire thawed it out. When the letter had become a limp and steaming thing, Jim stripped the flap of the envelope and carefully withdrew its contents.

DEAR MR HARLOW,

I am afraid I must disappoint you. I am in such a position, being an ex-convict, that I cannot afford to take the slightest risk. I will tell you frankly that what I have in my mind, is that this may be a frame-up organised by my friends the police, and I think that it would be, to say the least, foolish on my part to go any farther until I know your requirements, or at least have written proof that you have approached me.

Yours sincerely,
ARTHUR INGLE.

The two men looked at one another.

'That beats the band,' said Elk. 'What do you make of it, Carlton?'

Jim stood with his back to the fire, the letter in his hand, his brow wrinkled in a frown.

'I don't know . . . let me try now . . . Harlow asked Ingle to meet him: I knew that already. Ingle promised to go, changed his mind and wrote this letter, which has obviously never been opened by Harlow, and as obviously could not have been delivered to him before the interview, because, as I know – and I had a cold in the head to prove it – these two fellows met opposite the Horse Guards Parade and went joy-riding round the park for the greater part of an hour. Supposing Harlow is concerned with the slaying of this wretched woman – and why he should kill her heaven knows! – would he carry about this unopened letter and leave it for the first flat-footed policeman to find?'

He sat down in a chair and held his head in his hands, and presently:

'I've got it!' he said, his eyes blazing with excitement. 'At least, if I haven't got the whole story, I know at least one thing – poor Mrs Gibbins was very much in love with William Smith the platelayer!'

Elk stared at him.

'You're talking foolish,' he said.

11

AILEEN RIVERS had made one attempt to see her relative. She called up her uncle on the telephone and asked if she might call.

'Why?' was the uncompromising question.

Only a very pressing cause would have induced the girl to make the attempt – a fact which she conveyed to Ingle in the next sentence.

'I've had a big bill sent to me for the redecoration of your flat. You remember that you wished this done. The decorators hold me responsible—'

'Send the bill to me; I'll settle it,' he interrupted.

'I'm not sure that all the items are exact,' she began.

'It doesn't matter,' he broke in again. 'Send the bill: I'll settle it. Good morning.'

She hung up with a little smile, relieved of the necessity for another interview.

There were times when Aileen Rivers was extremely grateful that no drop of Arthur Ingle's blood ran in her veins. He had married her mother's first cousin, and the avuncular relationship was largely a complimentary one. She felt the need of emphasizing this fact upon Jim Carlton when he called that night – a very welcome visit, though he made it clear to her that the pleasure of seeing her again was not his sole object.

He had come to make inquiries which were a little inconsequent, she thought, about Mrs Gibbins. He seemed particularly anxious to know something about her nature, her qualities as a worker, and her willingness to undertake tasks which are as a rule outside the duties of a charwoman. She answered every question carefully and exactly, and when her examination had been completed:

'I won't ask you why you want to know all this,' she said,

'because I am sure that you must have a very good reason for asking. But I thought the case was finished?'

He shook his head.

'No murder is finished until the assassin is caught,' he said simply.

'It was murder?'

'I think so – Elk doesn't. Even the doctors at the inquest disagreed. There is just a remote possibility that it may have been an accident.' And then blandly: 'How is your attentive fellow-boarder?'

'Oh, Mr Brown?' she said with a smile. 'I don't know what has happened, but since I spoke to you I've hardly seen him. Yes, he is still staying at the house.'

His visit was disappointingly short, though in reality she should not have been disappointed, because she had brought home a lot of work from the office – Mr Stebbings was preparing his annual audit, and she had enough to keep her occupied till midnight. Yet she experienced a little twinge of unhappiness when Jim Carlton took an abrupt adieu. Though in no mood for work, she sat at her table until one o'clock, then, putting down her pen, opened the window and leaned out, inhaling the cold night air. The sky was clear and frosty; there was not a suspicion of the fog which had been predicted by the evening newspapers; and Coram Street was singularly peaceful and soothing. From time to time there came a distant whirr of wheels as cars and taxis passed along Theobald's Road, but this was the only jar in the harmony of silence. It was one of London's quiet nights. She looked up and down the street – the deserted pavement was very inviting. She was stiff and cramped through sitting too long in one position, and a quarter of an hour's walk was not only desirable, but necessary, she decided. Putting on her coat, she opened the door of her room and crept silently down the stairs, not wishing to disturb the other inmates of the house.

At the foot of the first flight of stairs she had a surprise. The door of the attentive boarder was wide open, and when she came abreast of it she saw him sitting in an armchair, a pipe gripped between his teeth, his hands clasped unromantically across his front and he was nodding sleepily. But she made sufficient noise to rouse him, and suddenly he sat up.

'Hullo!' he croaked, in the manner of one awaking from slumber. 'Are you going out?'

The impertinence of the man took her breath away.

'I thought of going for a stroll too,' he said, rising laboriously. 'I'm not getting enough exercise.'

'I'm going to post a letter, that is all,' she said; and had the humiliation of making a pretence to drop an imaginary letter into the pillar-box under his watchful eye.

She brushed past him as he stood in the doorway, blowing great clouds of smoke from his pipe, and almost ran up the stairs, angry with herself that she could allow so insignificant a thing to irritate her.

She did not see the man at breakfast, but as she walked up the steps to the office, she happened to glance round and, to her annoyance, saw him lounging on the corner of the square, apparently interested in nothing but the architecture of the fine old Queen Anne mansion which formed the corner block.

This day was to prove for Aileen Rivers something of an emotional strain. She was clearing up her desk preparatory to leaving the office when Mr Stebbings's bell rang. She went in with her notebook and pencil.

'No, no, no letter; I just have a curious request,' said Mr Stebbings, looking past her. 'A very curious and yet a very natural request. An old client of mine ... his secretary has a sore throat or something. He wanted to know if you'd go round after dinner and take a few letters.'

'Why certainly, Mr Stebbings,' she said, surprised that he should be so apologetic.

'He is not a client of mine now, as I think I've told you before,' the stout Mr Stebbings went on, addressing the chandelier. 'And I don't know that I should wish for him to be a client either. Only—'

'Mr Harlow?' she gasped, and he brought his gaze down to her level.

'Yes, Mr Harlow, 704 Park Lane. Do you mind?'

She shook her head.

'No,' she said. She had a struggle before she could agree. 'Why, of course I'll go. At what time?'

'He suggested nine. I said that was rather late, but he told me that he had a dinner engagement. He was most anxious,' said Mr Stebbings, his eyes returning to the Adam ceiling, 'that this matter should be kept as quiet as possible.'

'What matter?' she asked wonderingly.

'I don't know' – Mr Stebbings could be exasperatingly vague – 'I rather fancy it may have been the contents of the letter; or, on the other hand, it may have been that he did not wish anybody to know that he had a letter of such importance as would justify the calling in of a special stenographer to deal with it. Naturally I told him he might rely on your discretion ... thank you, that is all.'

She went back to her little room with the disquieting thought that she was committed to spend an hour alone with a man who on his last appearance had filled her with terror. She wondered whether she ought to tell Jim Carlton, and then she saw the absurdity of notifying to him every petty circumstance of her life, every coming and going. She knew he did not like Harlow; that he even suspected that splendid man of being responsible for the attack which had been made upon him in Long Acre; and she was the last to feed his prejudices. There were times when she allowed herself the disloyalty of thinking that Jim leaned a little towards sensationalism.

So she sent him no message, and at nine o'clock was ringing at the door of Mr Harlow's house.

She had not seen him since he came to the flat. Once he had passed her in his car, but only Jim had recognised him.

Aileen was curious to discover whether she would recover that impression of power he had conveyed on the night of his call; whether the same thrill of fear would set her pulses beating faster – or whether on second view he would shrink to the proportions of someone who was just removed from the commonplace.

She had not anticipated that it would be Harlow himself who would open the door to her. He wore a dinner jacket, a pleated silk shirt and round the waist of his well cut trousers a cummerbund of oriental brocade. He looked superb. But the old thrill? . . .

Without realising her action she shook her head slowly.

His was a tremendous personality, dominating, masterful, sublimely confident. But he was not god-like. Almost she felt disappointed. Yet if he had been the Harlow of her mind it is doubtful whether she would have entered the house.

'Most good of you!' He helped her to struggle out of her heavy coat. 'And very good of Stebbings! The truth is that my secretary is down with 'flu and I hate employing people from agencies.'

He opened the door of the library and entering, stood waiting with the edge of the door in his hand. As she stepped into the library, her foot slipped from under her on the highly-polished floor, and she would have fallen, but he caught her in a grip that was surprisingly fierce. As she recovered, she was facing him, and she saw something like horror in his eyes – just a glimpse, swift to come and go.

'This floor is dreadful,' he said jerkily. 'The men from Herrans should have been here to lay the carpet.'

She uttered an incoherent apology for her clumsiness, but he would not listen.

'No, no – unless you are used to the trick of walking on it—'

His concern was genuine, but he made a characteristic recovery.

'I have a very important letter to write – a most important letter. And I am the worst of writers! Dictation is a cruel habit to acquire – the dictator becomes the slave of his typist!'

His attitude might be described as being genially off-handed. It struck Aileen that he was not at all anxious to impress her. She missed the smirk and the touch of ingratiating pomposity with which the middle-aged business man seeks to establish an impression upon a new and pretty stenographer. In a sense he was brusque, though he was always pleasant. She had the feeling of being put in her place – but it was an exact grading – she was in the place she belonged, no higher, no lower.

'You have a notebook? Good! Will you sit at my table? I belong to the peripatetic school of dictators. Comfortable? Now—'

He gave a name and an address, spelling them carefully. The letter was to a Colonel Harry Mayburgh of 9003 Wall Street.

My dear Harry, he began. The dictation went smoothly from hereon. Harlow's diction was a little slow but distinct. He was never once at a loss for a word, nor did he flounder in the morass of parentheses. Towards the end of the letter:

. . . the European situation remains settled and there is every promise of a revival in trade during the next few months. I, for one, will never believe that so unimportant a matter as the Bonn affair will cause the slightest friction between ourselves and the French.

She remembered now reading of the incident. A quarrel between a *sous-officier* of the French army and a peppery British colonel who had gone to Bonn.

So unimportant was the incident that when a question had been raised in the House of Commons by an inquisitive member, he had been greeted by jeering laughter. It seemed surprising that a man of Harlow's standing should think it worth while to make any reference to the incident.

He stopped here, pinching his chin and gazing down at her abstractedly. She met the pale eyes – was conscious that in some ineffable manner his appearance had undergone a change.

The pale eyes were deeper set; they seemed to have receded, leaving two little wrinkles of flesh to spoil the unmarked smoothness of skin. Perhaps she was mistaken and was seeing now, in a leisurely survey, characteristics which had been overlooked in the shock of meeting him at Fotheringay Mansions. ...

'Yes,' he said slowly, answering, as it were, a question he had put to himself. 'I think I might say that. Will you read back?'

She read the letter from her shorthand and when she had finished he smiled.

'Splendid!' he said quietly. 'I envy Mr Stebbings so efficient a young lady.'

He walked to the side-table, lifted a typewriter and carried it to the desk.

'You will find paper and carbons in the top right hand drawer,' he said. 'Would you mind waiting for me after you have finished? I shall not be more than twenty minutes.'

She had made the required copies of the letter within a few minutes of his departure. There were certain matters to be considered; she sat back, her hands folded lightly on her lap, her eyes roving the room.

Mr Harlow's splendour showed inoffensively in the decorations of the room. The furniture, even the bookcases which covered the walls, were in Empire style. There was a pervading sense of richness in the room and yet it might not in truth be called over-ornate, despite the gold and crystal of the candelabras, the luxury of heavy carpets and silken damask.

So roving her eyes came to the fire-place where the red coals were dying. On the white-tiled hearth immediately before the fire a little screw of paper had been thrown which, under the influence of the heat, had opened into a crumpled ball. She saw a pencilled scrawl.

'Marling.'

She spelt the word – thought at first it was 'making.' And then she did something which shocked her even in the act – she stooped and picked up the paper, smoothed it out and read quickly, as though she must satisfy her curiosity before her outraged sense of propriety intervened.

I really must ask for my writing material. Please leave me that. How can I prepare my history?

MARLING.

The handle of the door turned; she slipped the creased paper into her bag which was open on the table and closed it as the stony-faced Mrs Edwins came into the room.

She came to the desk where the girl sat, her big, gaunt hands folded, her disparagement conveyed rather than expressed.

'You're the young woman,' she stated.

'I'm the young woman,' smiled Aileen, who had a soft spot for age.

She grew a little uncomfortable under the silent scrutiny that followed.

'You're a typewriter?'

'A typist – yes. I am Mr Stebbings's secretary.'

'Stebbings!'

Mrs Edwins' voice was surprisingly harsh and loud. The sudden change which came to her face was remarkable. Eyes and thin lips opened together in startled surprise.

'Stebbings? The lawyer? You've come here from him?'

For a second the girl was too startled to reply.

'Yes ... Mr Harlow asked that I be sent; his secretary was ill—'

'Oh – that's it!' Relief unmistakable.

And here it flashed on the girl that this must be Mrs Edwins – that L. Edwins to whom reference had been made in the will of the late Miss Mercy Harlow. Perhaps, her nerves on edge, the woman received the thought, for she said quickly:

'I am Mrs Lucy Edwins – Mr Harlow's housekeeper.'

Aileen murmured some polite commonplace and wondered what was coming next. Nothing apparently, for, with a quick glance round the room, the woman sailed out, her hands still clasped before her, leaving the girl to her penitence and self-reproach. And these distresses were inevitable. A prying maid (she told herself) who read her mistress's letters and poked into the mysteries of locked drawers was a pattern of decorum compared with a secretary who yet must inspect the waste-paper of a chance employer. She was of a mind to throw the paper into the fire, but it was natural that she should find excuses for her conduct. And her excuse (stoutly offered and defended to herself) was Jim Carlton and the vague familiarity of 'Marling'.

Ten minutes passed and then Mr Harlow came slowly into the room. The door closed with a click behind him and he stood before her on the very spot where Mrs Edwins had conducted her cold survey.

'My housekeeper came in, didn't she?'

'Yes'. She wondered what was coming next.

'My housekeeper' – he spoke slowly – 'is the most unbalanced female I have ever known! She is the most suspicious woman I have ever known; and the most annoying woman I am ever likely to know.'

His eyes did not leave her face.

'I wonder if you know why I sent for you?'

The question took her aback for the moment.

'Don't say to write a letter,' he smiled. 'I really wanted no letter written! It was an excuse to get you here alone for a little talk. And the fact that you have not gone pale and that you display no visible evidence of agitation is very pleasing to me. If you had, I should have opened the door to you and bid you a polite good night.'

He waited for her to speak.

'I don't quite understand what you want, Mr Harlow.'

'Really? I was afraid that you would – and understand wrongly!'

He strode up and down the library, his hands under his coat tails, his head lifted so that he seemed immediately interested in the cornice.

'I want a view – an angle. I can't get that from any commonplace person. You are not commonplace. You are not brilliant either – forgive my frankness. You're a woman, perhaps in love – perhaps not. I don't know, but a normal soul. You have no interest to serve.'

He stopped abruptly, looked at her, pointing to the door.

'That door is locked,' he said. 'There is nobody in this

90

house but myself and my housekeeper. The telephone near your right hand is disconnected. I am very fond of you!'

He paused and then nodded approvingly.

'A little colour – that is annoyance. No trembling – that may come later. Will you be so good as to press the bell – you will find it ... yes, that is it.'

Mechanically she had obeyed, and almost immediately the door opened and a tall manservant came in.

'I want you to wait in the servants' hall until this young lady has gone, Thomas – I have a letter I wish posted.'

The man bowed and went out. Mr Harlow smiled.

'That disproves two statements I made to you – that the door was locked and that we were alone in the house. Now I think I know you! I wasn't certain before. And of course I'm not fond of you – I like you though. If you feel inclined to call up James Carlton, the telephone is through to the exchange.'

'Will you please tell me,' she said quietly, 'what all this means?'

He stood by the desk now, his white fingers beating a noiseless tattoo.

'I know you, that is the point,' he said. 'I can now speak to you very plainly. Would you, for a very large financial consideration, marry a man in whom I am greatly interested?'

She shook her head and he approved even of the refusal.

'That is splendid! You did not say I was insulting you, or that you could not marry a man for money – none of the clichés of the film or the novelette! You would have disappointed me if you had.'

Aileen made a discovery that left her doubting her own sanity. She liked this man. She believed in his sincerity. A crooked dealer he might be, but upon a plane which was beyond her comprehension. In the less lofty regions in the levels of human intercourse he was beyond suspicion. She felt curiously safe with him and was worried, as one who was in the process of changing a settled opinion in the face of a prejudiced habit of thought.

He had the face of a materialist – the blue of his eyes was (Jim had told her) common to great generals and great murderers. The thick lips and fleshy nose were repellent. Yet she lived consciously in a world of men and women – she did not look for god or hero in any man. None was wholly good; none was wholly bad, except in the most artificial of dramas.

'I wonder if I know what you are thinking about?'

She mistrusted him now, having a sense of his uncanny power of mind-reading.

'You are saying "I wonder if he is as great a scoundrel as people like Carlton say?" How shall you measure me? It is very difficult, not because I represent greatness, but because the canvas on which I work is immense. Miss Rivers, I hoped that you were heart-free.'

'I think I am,' she said.

'Which means that you are not. I wanted you to marry somebody I love; the sweetest nature in the world. Something I have created out of confusion and chaos and shining lights and mysterious sounds. I talk like a divinity, but it is true. For years I have been looking for a wife.'

He leaned forward over the desk and his voice sank.

'Shall I tell you something?'

And though she made no sign, he read her interest aright.

'If you had said "yes", my day would have been done. I am selfishly relieved that you declined. But if it had been "yes", all this would have crumbled into dust – all the splendours of the Splendid Harlow! Dust and memories and failure!'

For a moment she thought he had been drinking and that she had not detected his condition before. But he was sober enough and very, very sane.

'Strange, isn't it? I like you. I like Carlton – unscrupulous but a nice man. He is waiting outside this house for you. Also a fellow-lodger of yours, a Mr Brown, who followed you here.'

She gasped at this.

'He is a detective. Carlton is scared for you – he suspects me of harbouring the most sinister plans.' His chuckle had a rich music in it. 'Maybe I can help you some time. I'd love to give you a million and see what you would do with it.'

He held out his hand, and she took it without hesitation.

'You haven't told me whom I was to marry?'

'A man with a golden beard,' he laughed. 'Forgive my little joke!'

She went out of the house bewildered and stopped on the step with a cry of wonder. Jim Carlton was standing on the sidewalk; and with him was Mr Brown, her fellow-boarder.

Mr Harlow waited until the door had closed upon his visitor and was stepping into the lift when his yellow-faced housekeeper appeared noiselessly from the direction of the servants' hall.

'What did that girl want?' she asked.

'Liberty of action,' he replied.

'I don't understand what you're talking about half the time,' she complained. 'I wouldn't be surprised if she wasn't a spy.'

'Nothing would surprise you, my dear woman,' he said, his hand on the grille of the elevator.

'I don't like the look of her.'

'I, on the contrary, like the look of her very much.' He was resigned to the conversation. 'I asked her to marry.'

'You!' she almost screamed.

'No.' He jerked his head to the ceiling and broke in upon her violent comment. 'I'm not mad. I am very clever. I can face truth – that is the cleverest thing any man can do. I'm going up to Saul Marling.'

Her shrill voice followed him up the elevator shaft.

'Fantastical nonsense ... wasting your time!'

He closed the door of Marling's apartment behind him and sank into a deep chair with a groan of relief. The bearded man, his face shadowed by a reading shade, looked round, chin on palm.

'She has a tantrum today,' he said, nodding his head

wisely. 'She was quite rude when I complained about the fish.'

'The devil she was!' Harlow sat upright, was on the point of rising but thought better of it. 'You must have what you wish, my dear Saul. I will raise Cain if you don't. What are you reading?'

Marling turned over the book to assure himself of the title. '*The Interpretation of Dreams*,' he read.

'Freud! Chuck it in the waste-paper basket,' scoffed Harlow.

'I don't understand it very well,' admitted his companion.

'The man who can interpret other people's dreams can interpret other people's thought,' said Harlow. 'I have been dreaming for you, Saul Marling. I dreamt a wife for you, but she would have none of it.'

'A wife!' said the startled Marling, his hand trembling in his agitation. 'I don't want a wife – you know that!'

Mr Harlow lit a cigar.

'Yes – but she doesn't want a husband – I know *that*! Dreams, huh?'

He laughed to himself, the other man watching him curiously.

'Do you ever dream?' he asked with a timidity which was almost pathetic.

'I? Lord, yes! I dream of jokes.'

Marling could not understand this: this strong man had talked about 'jokes' before, and when they were elaborated they had not amused anybody but Mr Harlow.

It is a peculiar trait of the English criminal that he never describes his unlawful act or acts by grandiloquent terms. Crime of all kind, especially crime against the person, is a 'joke'. The man who holds up a cashier has 'had a joke with him'; the confidence swindler 'jokes' his victim; a warehouse theft would be modestly described in the same way.

Mr Stratford Harlow once heard the term employed and never forgot it. This cant phrase so nearly covered his own

94

mental attitude towards his operations; a good joke would produce the same emotions of mind and body.

Once he had written to an important rubber house offering to take its entire stock at a price which would show a fair profit to the seller. The house and its affiliated concerns smelt a forced buying and the price of rubber rose artificially. He waited three months, buying everywhere but from the united companies and one night their stores illuminated the shipping of the Mersey.

That was a very good joke indeed. Mr Harlow chuckled for days, not because he had made an enormous fortune – the joke had to be there or the money had no value.

'I don't like your jokes,' said Marling gravely.

'I shouldn't tell you about them,' said Mr Harlow, suppressing a yawn; 'but I have no secrets from you, Saul Marling. And I love testing them against your magnificent honesty. If you laughed at them as I laugh, I'd be worried sick. Come along to the roof for your walk and I'll tell you the greatest joke of all. It starts with a dinner-party given in this house and ends with somebody making twenty millions and living happily ever after!'

It required a perceptible effort in Aileen to produce the paper she had found in the grate of Mr Harlow's library. She had the unhappy knowledge that whilst this big man had put her in her place, she hadn't stayed there. She had gone down into deplorable depths. He might be anything that Jim believed, but on his own plane he had a claim to greatness.

When she reached that conclusion she felt that it was time to hand the paper to her companion.

'I'm not going to excuse myself,' she said frankly. 'It was an abominable thing to do, and I won't even say that I had you in my mind. It was just vulgar curiosity made me do it.'

They stopped under a street lamp and he opened the paper and read the message.

'Marling!' he gasped. 'Good God!'

'What is it?'

The effect of those scribbled words upon her companion astounded her. Presently he folded the paper very carefully and put it in his pocket.

'Marling, Ingle, Mrs Gibbins,' he said, in his old bantering mood. 'Put me together the pieces of this jigsaw puzzle; and connect if you can the note of this Mr Marling, who wishes to retain his writing materials; your disreputable uncle who has developed a craze for film projecting; fit in the piece which stands for Mrs Gibbins and her beloved William Smith; explain a certain letter that was never posted and never delivered, yet was found in a frozen puddle – I nearly said puzzle! – and make of all these one intelligible picture.'

'What on earth are you talking about?' she asked helplessly.

He shook his head.

'You don't know! Elk doesn't know. I'm not so sure that I know, but I wish the next ten days were through!'

12

FOR SOME reason which she could not explain to herself, Aileen was irritated.

'Do you realise how horribly mysterious you are?' she asked, almost tartly. 'I always thought that the mystery of detectives was an illusion fostered by sensational writers.'

'All mystery is illusion,' he said grandly.

They had reached Oxford Street.

'Have you ever been to the House of Commons?' he asked her suddenly.

She shook her head.

'No.'

'Then come along. You'll see something more entertaining than a film or a play, but you will hear very little that hasn't been said better elsewhere.'

The House was in session, though she was only dimly aware of this, for she belonged to the large majority of people to whom the workings of Parliament were a closed book. Jim, on the contrary, was extraordinarily well informed in political affairs and favoured her with a brief dissertation on the subject. The old hard and fast party spirit was moribund, he said. The electorate had grown too flexible for any machine to control. There had been surprising results in recent by-elections to illustrate a fact so disconcerting to party organizers. The present Government, she learnt, despite its large majority, was on its last legs. There was dissension within the Cabinet; and rebel caves honeycombed the Government party.

In truth she was only faintly interested. But the approach to the Commons was impressive. The lofty hall, the broad stairway, the echoing lobby with its hurrying figures, and the mystery of what lay behind the door at one end, brought her a new thrill.

Jim disappeared and returned with a ticket. They passed up a flight of stairs and presently she was admitted to one of the galleries.

Her first impression was one of disappointment. The House was so much smaller than she had expected. Somebody was talking; a pale bald man, who rocked and swayed slowly as he delivered himself of a monotonous and complaining tirade on the failure of the Government to do something or other about the Basingstoke Canal. There were only a few dozen members in the House, and mainly they were engaged in talking or listening to one another, and apparently taking no notice of the speaker. On the front bench three elderly men sat, head to head, in consultation. Mr Speaker in his canopied chair seemed the only person who was taking a keen interest in the member's oration.

Even as she looked, the House began to fill. A ceaseless procession of men trooped in and took their places on the benches, stopping as they passed to exchange a word with somebody already seated. The orator still droned on; and then Jim pressed her arm and nodded.

From behind the Speaker's chair had come a man whom she instantly recognised as Sir Joseph Layton, the Foreign Minister. He was in evening dress except that he wore, instead of the conventional dinner jacket, one of black velvet. He sat down on the front bench, fingered his tiny white moustache with a characteristic gesture, and then the member who had been speaking sat down. Somebody rose from one of the front benches and asked a question which did not reach the girl. Sir Joseph jerked to his feet, his hands gripping the lapels of his velvet coat, his head on one side like an inquisitive sparrow, and she listened without hearing to his reply. His voice was husky; he had a dozen odd mannerisms of speech and gesture that fascinated her. And then Jim's hand touched her.

'I'm going down to see him. Will you wait for me in the lobby?' he whispered and she nodded.

It was ten minutes before the Foreign Minister came out of the House, greeted the detective with a wave of his hand and put his arm in Jim's.

'Well, what is the news?' he asked, when they reached his private room. 'Harlow again, eh? Something dark and sinister going on in international circles of diplomacy?'

He chuckled at the joke as he sat down at his big table and filled his pipe from a tin of tobacco that stood at his elbow.

'Harlow, Harlow!' he said, with good-humoured impatience. 'Everybody is telling me about Harlow! I'm going to have a talk with the fellow. He is giving a dinner-party on Tuesday and I've promised to look in before I come to the House.'

'What is the excuse for the dinner?' asked Jim, interested.

The Minister laughed.

'He is a secret diplomatist, if you like. He has fixed up a very unpleasant little quarrel which might have developed in the Middle East – really it amounted to a row between two bloodthirsty brigands! – and he is giving a sort of olive-branch dinner to the ambassadors of the two states concerned. I can't go to the dinner, but I shall go to the reception afterwards. Well,' he asked abruptly, 'what is your news?'

'I came here to get news, not to give it, Sir Joseph,' said Jim. 'That well-known cloud is not developing?'

'Pshaw!' said the Minister impatiently. 'Cloud!'

'The Bonn incident?' suggested Jim, and Sir Joseph exploded.

'There was no incident! It was a vulgar slanging match between an elderly and pompous staff colonel and an impudent puppy of a French *sous-officier!* The young man has been disciplined by the French, and the colonel has been relieved of his post by the War Office. And that is the end of a so-called incident.'

Jim rejoined the girl soon after and learnt that Parliament had not greatly impressed her. Perhaps her mood was to blame that she found him a rather dull companion; for the rest of the evening, whilst she was with him, she did most of the talking, and he replied either in monosyllables or not at all. She understood him well enough to suspect that something unusual must have happened and did not banter him on his long silence.

At the door of her boarding-house he asked:

'You won't object to Brown staying on?'

'I intended speaking about him,' she said. 'Why am I under observation – that is the term, isn't it?'

'But do you mind?'

'No,' she said, shaking her head. 'It is rather funny.'

'A sense of humour is a great thing,' he replied, and that was his farewell.

Elk was not at Scotland Yard. He went up to the Great Eastern Road, where the inspector had rooms; and he was distinctly piqued to learn that Elk knew all about the Harlow dinner.

'I only got to know this afternoon, though,' said Elk. 'If

you'd been at the Yard I could have told you – the thing was only organised yesterday. We shouldn't have heard anything about it, but Harlow applied for two policemen to be on duty outside the house. Swift worker, Harlow.' His small eyes surveyed Jim Carlton gravely. 'Tell you something else, son: Ratas have bought up a new office building in Moorgate Street. I forget the name of the fellow who bought it. Anyway, Ellenbury took over yesterday – got in double staff. He is a fellow you might see.'

'He is a fellow I intend seeing,' said Jim. 'What is he now – lawyer or financier?'

'A lawyer. But he knows as much about finance as law. I've got an idea he's on the crook. We've never had a complaint against him, though there was a whisper once about his financial position. In the old days he used to act for some mighty queer people; and I think he lost money on the Stock Exchange.'

'He's the man who lives at Norwood?'

Elk nodded.

'Norwood,' he said deliberately; 'the place where the letters were posted to Mrs Gibbins. I wondered you hadn't seen him before – no, I haven't, though.' He reconsidered. 'You didn't want to make Harlow think that you are on to that Gibbins business.' He stroked his nose thoughtfully. 'Yuh, that's it. He doesn't know you. You might call on him on some excuse, but you'll have to be careful.'

'How does he get from Norwood to the City?'

Elk shook his head.

'He's not the kind of fellow you can pick up in the train,' he said. 'He runs a hired car which Ratas pay for. Royalton House is his address. It's an old brick box near the Crystal Palace. He lives there with his wife – an invalid. He hasn't any vices that I know of, unless being a friend of Harlow's puts him on the list. And he's not approachable any other way. He doesn't work in Norwood, but has a little office in Theobald's Road; and if you call his clerk will see you and tell you that he is very sorry but Mr Ellenbury can't give you an appointment for the next ten years! But Ellenbury might tell something, if you could get at him.'

'You are certain that Ellenbury is working with Harlow?'

'Working with him?' Elk spat contemptuously but unerringly into the fire. 'I should say he was! They're like brothers – up to a point. Do you remember the police station old man Harlow presented to a grateful nation! It was Ellenbury who bought the ground and gave the orders to the builders. Nobody knew it was a police station until it was up. After they'd put in the foundations and got the walls breast-high, there was a sort of strike because foreign labour was employed, and all the workmen had to be sent back to Italy or Germany, or wherever they came from. That's where Ellenbury's connection came under notice, though we weren't aware that he was working for Harlow till a year later.'

Jim decided upon taking the bolder course, but the lawyer was prepared for the visitation.

13

Mr ELLENBURY had his home in a large, gaunt house between Norwood and Anerley. It had been ugly even in the days when square, box-shaped dwellings testified to the strange mentality of the Victorian architects and stucco was regarded as an effective and artistic method of covering bad brickwork. It was in shape a cube, from the low centre of which, on the side facing the road, ran a long flight of stone steps confined within a plaster balustrade. It had oblong windows set at regular intervals on three sides, and was a mansion to which even venetian blinds lent an air of distinction.

Royalton House stood squarely in the centre of two acres of land, and could boast a rosery, a croquet lawn, a kitchen garden, a rustic summer-house and a dribbling fountain. Scattered about the grounds there were a number of indelicate statues representing famous figures of mythology – these had been purchased cheaply from a local exhibition many years before at a great weeding-out of those gods chiselled with such anatomical faithfulness that they constituted an offence to the eye of the Young Person.

In such moments of leisure as his activities allowed, Mr Ellenbury occupied a room gloomily papered, which was variously styled 'The Study', and 'The Master's Room' by his wife and his domestic staff. It was a high and ill-proportioned apartment, cold and cheerless in the winter, and was overcrowded with furniture that did not fit. Round tables and top-heavy secretaires; a horsehair sofa that ran askew across one corner of the room, where it could only be reached by removing a heavy card-table; there was space for Mr Ellenbury to sit and little more.

On this December evening he sat at his roll-top desk, biting his nails thoughtfully, a look of deep concern on his pinched face. He was a man who had grown prematurely old in a lifelong struggle to make his resources keep pace with ambition. He was a lover of horses; not other people's horses that show themselves occasionally on a race track, but horses to keep in one's own stable, horses that looked over the half-door at the sound of a familiar voice; horses that might be decked in shiny harness shoulder to shoulder and draw a glittering phaeton along a country road.

All men have their dreams; for forty years Mr Ellenbury's pet dream had been to drive into the arena of a horse show behind two spanking bays with nodding heads and high knee action, and to drive out again amidst the plaudits of the multitude with the ribbons of the first prize streaming from the bridles of his team. Many a man has dreamt less worthily.

He had had bad luck with his horses, bad luck with his family. Mrs Ellenbury was an invalid. No doctor had ever discovered the nature of her illness. One West End specialist had seen her and had advised the calling in of another. The second specialist had suggested that it would be advisable to see a third. The third had come and asked questions. Had any of her parents suffered from illusions? Were they hysterical? Didn't Mrs Ellenbury think that if she made an effort she could get up from her bed for, say, half an hour a day?

The truth was that Mrs Ellenbury, having during her life experienced most of the sensations which are peculiar to womankind, having walked and worked, directed servants, given little parties, made calls, visited the theatre, played croquet and tennis, had decided some twenty years ago that there was nothing quite as comfortable as staying in bed. So she became an invalid, had a treble subscription at a library and acquired a very considerable acquaintance with the rottenness of society, as depicted by authors who were authorities on misunderstood wives.

In a sense Mr Ellenbury was quite content that this condition of affairs should be as it was. Once he was satisfied that his wife, in whom he had the most friendly interest, was suffering no pain, he was satisfied to return to the bachelor life. Every morning and every night (when he returned home at a reasonable hour) he went into her room and asked:

'How are we today?'

'About the same – certainly no worse.'

'That's fine! Is there anything you want?'

'No, thank you – I have everything.'

This exchange varied slightly from day to day, but generally it followed on those lines.

Ellenbury had come back late from Ratas after a tiring day. Usually he directed the Rata Syndicate from his own office; indeed, he had never before appeared visibly in the operations of the company. But this new coup of Harlow's was on so gigantic a scale that he must appear in the daylight; and his connection with a concern suspected by every reputable firm in the City must be public property. And that hurt him. He, who had secretly robbed his clients, who had engaged in systematic embezzlement and might now, but for the intervention and help of Mr Stratford Harlow, have been an inmate of Dartmoor, walked with shame under the stigma of his known connection with a firm which was openly described as unsavoury.

He was a creature of Harlow, his slave. This sore place in his self-esteem had never healed. It was his recreation to brood upon the ignominy of his lot. He hated Harlow with a malignity that none, seeing his mild, worn face, would suspect.

To him Stratford Harlow was the very incarnation of evil, a devil on earth who had bound his soul in fetters of brass. And of late he had embarked upon a novel course of dreaming. It was the confused middle of a dream, having neither beginning nor end, but it was all about a humiliated Harlow; Harlow being dragged in chains through the Awful Arch; Harlow robbed at the apotheosis of his triumph. And always Ellenbury was there, leering, chuckling, pointing a derisive finger at the man he had ruined, or else he was flitting by midnight across the Channel with a suitcase packed with fabulous sums of money that he had filched from his master.

Mr Ellenbury bit his nails.

Soon money would be flowing into Ratas – he would spend days endorsing cheques, clearing drafts ... drafts ...

You may pass a draft into a bank and it becomes a number of figures in a pass-book. On the other hand, you may hand it across the counter and receive real money. Sometimes Harlow preferred that method – dollars into sterling, sterling into Swiss francs, Swiss francs into florins, until the identity of the original payment was beyond recognition.

Drafts ...

In the room above his head his wife was lying immersed in the self-revelations of a fictional countess. Mrs Ellenbury had little money of her own. The house was her property. He could augment her income by judicious remittances.

Drafts. ...

Mauve and blue and red. 'Pay to the order of—' so many thousand dollars, or rupees, or yen.

Harlow never interfered. He gave exact instructions as to how the money was to be dealt with, into which accounts it must be paid and that was all. At the end of a transaction he threw a thousand or two at his assistant, as a bone to a dog.

Ellenbury had never been so rich in his life as he was now. He could meet his bank manager without a sinking feeling in the pit of his stomach – no longer did the sight of a strange man walking up the drive to the house fill him with a sense of foreboding. Yet once he had seen the sheriff's officer in every stranger.

But he had grown accustomed to prosperity; it had become a normal condition of life and freed his mind to hate the source of his affluence.

A slave – at best a freedman. If Harlow crooked his finger he must run to him; if Harlow on a motoring tour wired 'Meet me at—' any inaccessible spot, he must drop his work and hurry there. He, Franklin Ellenbury, an officer of the High Court of Justice, a graduate of a great university, a man of sensibility and genius.

No wonder Mr Ellenbury bit at his nails and thought of drafts and sunny cafés and picture galleries which he had long desired to visit; and perhaps, after he was sated with the novelty of travel, a villa near Florence with orange groves and masses of bougainvillaea clustering between white walls and jade-green jalousies.

'A gentleman to see you, sir.'

He aroused himself from his dreams with a painful start.

'To see me?' The clock on his desk said fifteen minutes after eleven. All the house save the weary maid was asleep. 'But at this hour? Who is he? What does he want?'

'He's outside, in a big car.'

Automatically he sprang to his feet and ran out of the room.

Harlow!

How like the swine, not condescending to alight, but summoning his Thing to his chariot wheels!

'Is that you, Ellenbury?'

The voice that spoke from the darkness of the car was his.

'Yes, Mr Harlow.'

'You'll be getting inquiries about the Gibbins woman – probably tomorrow. Carlton is certain to call – he has found that the letters were posted from Norwood. Why didn't you post them in town?'

'I thought – er – well, I wanted to keep the business away from my office.'

'You could still have posted them in town. Don't try to hide up the fact that you sent those letters. Mrs Gibbins was an old family servant of yours. You told me once that you had a woman with a similar name in your employ—'

'She's dead—' began Ellenbury.

'So much the easier for you to lie!' was the answer. 'Is everything going smoothly at Ratas?'

'Everything, Mr Harlow.'

'Good!'

The lawyer stood at the foot of the steps watching the carmine rear light of the car until it vanished on the road.

That was Harlow! Requesting nothing – just ordering. Saying 'Let this be done,' and never doubting that it would be done.

He went slowly back to his study, dismissed the servant to bed; and until the early hours of the morning was studying a continental timetable – Madrid, Munich, Cordova, Bucharest – delightful places all.

As he passed his wife's bedroom she called him and he went in.

'I'm not at all well tonight,' she said fretfully. 'I can't sleep.'

He comforted her with words, knowing that at ten o'clock that night she had eaten a supper that would have satisfied an agricultural labourer.

14

Mr HARLOW had timed his warning well. He had the general's gift of foretelling his enemy's movements. Jim called the next morning at the lawyer's office in Theobald's Road; and when the dour clerk denied him an interview, he produced his card.

'Take that to Mr Ellenbury. I think he will see me,' he said.

The clerk returned in a few seconds and ushered him into a cupboard of a place which could not have been more than seven feet square. Mr Ellenbury rose nervously from behind his microscopic desk and offered a limp, damp hand.

'Good morning, Inspector,' he said. 'We do not get many visitors from Scotland Yard. May I inquire your business?'

'I am making inquiries regarding the death of a woman named Gibbins,' said the visitor.

Mr Ellenbury was not startled. He bowed his head slowly.

'She was the woman taken out of the Regent's Canal some weeks ago; I remember the inquest,' he said.

'Her mother, Louise Gibbins, had been drawing a quarterly pension of thirteen pounds, which, I understand, was sent by you?'

It was a bluff designed to startle the man into betraying himself but, to Jim Carlton's astonishment, Mr Ellenbury lowered his head again.

'Yes,' he said, 'that is perfectly true. I knew her mother, a very excellent old lady who was for some time in my employ. She was very good to my dear wife, who is an invalid, and I have made her an allowance for many years. I did not know she was dead until the case of the drowned charwoman came into court and caused me to make inquiries.'

'The allowance was stopped before these facts were made public,' challenged Jim Carlton, and again he was dumbfounded when the lawyer agreed.

'It was delayed – not stopped,' he said, 'and it was only by accident that the money was not sent at the usual time. Fortunately or unfortunately, I happened to be rather ill when the allowance should have been sent off. The day I returned to the office and dispatched the money I learnt of Mrs Gibbins's death. It is clear that the woman, instead of informing me of her mother's death, suppressed the fact in order that she might benefit financially. If she had lived and it had come to my notice, I should naturally have prosecuted her for embezzlement.'

Carlton knew that his visit had been anticipated, and the story cut and dried in advance. To press any further questions would be to make Harlow's suspicion a certainty. He could round off his inquiry plausibly enough, and this he did.

'I think that is my final question in the case,' he said with a smile. 'I am sorry to have bothered you, Mr Ellenbury. You never met Mrs Annie Gibbins?'

'Never,' replied Ellenbury, with such emphasis that Jim knew he was speaking the truth. 'I assure you I had no idea of her existence.'

From one lawyer to another was a natural step: more natural since Mr Stebbings' office was in the vicinity, and this interview at least held one pleasant possibility – he might see Aileen.

She was a little staggered when he entered her room. 'Mr Stebbings! – why on earth—?' And then penitently: 'I'm so sorry! I am not as inquisitive as I appear!'

Mr Stebbings, who was surprised at nothing, saw him at once and listened without comment to the detective's business.

'I never saw Mr Marling except once,' he said. 'He was a wild, rather erratic individual, and as far as I know, went to the Argentine and did not return.'

'You're sure that he went abroad?' asked Jim.

Mr Stebbings, being a lawyer, was too cautious a man to be sure of anything.

'He took his ticket and presumably sailed; his name was on the passenger list. Miss Alice Harlow caused inquiries to be made; I think she was most anxious that Marling's association with Mr Harlow should be definitely broken. That, I am afraid, is all I can tell you.'

'What kind of man was Marling? Yes, I know he was wild and a little erratic, but was he the type of man who could be dominated by Harlow?'

A very rare smile flitted across the massive face of the lawyer.

'Is there anybody in the world who would not be dominated by Mr Harlow?' he asked dryly. 'I know very little of what is happening outside my own profession, but from such knowledge as I have acquired I understand that Mr Harlow is rather a tyrant. I use the word in its original and historic sense,' he hastened to add.

Jim made a gentle effort to hear more about Mr Harlow and his earlier life. He was particularly interested in the will, a copy of which he had evidently seen at Somerset House, but here the lawyer was adamant. He hinted that, if the police procured an order from a judge in chambers, or if they went through some obscure process of law, he would have no alternative but to reveal all that he knew about his former client; otherwise—

Aileen was not in her room when he passed through, and he lingered awhile, hoping to see her, but apparently she was engaged (to her annoyance, it must be confessed) with the junior partner; he left Bloomsbury with a feeling that he had not extracted the completest satisfaction from his visits.

At the corner of Bedford Place a blue Rolls was drawn up by the sidewalk, and so deep was he in thought that he would have passed, had not the man who was sitting at the wheel removed the long cigar from his white teeth and called him by name. Jim turned with a start. The last person he expected to meet at this hour of the morning in the prosaic environment of Theobald's Road.

'I thought it was you.' Mr Harlow's voice was cheerful, his manner a pattern of geniality. 'This is a fortunate meeting.'

'For which of us!' smiled Jim, leaning his elbow on the window opening and looking into the face of the man.

'For both, I hope. Come inside, and I'll drive you anywhere you're going. I have an invitation to offer and a suggestion to make.'

Jim opened the door and stepped in. Harlow was a skilful driver. He slipped in and out of the traffic into Bedford Square, and then:

'Do you mind if I drive you to my house? Perhaps you can spare the time?'

Jim nodded, wondering what was the proposition. But throughout the drive Mr Harlow kept up a flow of unimportant small talk, and he said nothing important until he showed his visitor into the beautiful library. Mr Harlow threw his heavy coat and cap on to one of the red settees, twisted a chair round, so that it revolved like a teetotum, and set it down near his visitor.

'Somebody followed you here,' he said. 'I saw him out of the tail of my eye. A Scotland Yard man! My dear man, you are very precious to the law.' He chuckled at this. 'But I bear you no malice that you do not trust me! My theory is that it is much better for a dozen innocent men to come under police surveillance than for a guilty man to escape detection. Only it is sometimes a little unnerving, the knowledge that I am being watched. I could stop it at once, of course. The *Courier* is in the market – I could buy a newspaper and make your lives very unpleasant indeed. I could raise a dozen men up in Parliament to ask what the devil you meant by it. In fact, my dear Carlton, there are so many ways of breaking you and your immediate superior that I cannot carry them in my head!'

And Jim had an uncomfortable feeling that this was no vain boast.

'I really don't mind,' Harlow went on; 'it annoys me a little, but amuses me more. I am almost above the law! How stupid that sounds!' He slapped his knee and his rich laughter filled the room. 'Of course I am; you know that! Unless I do something very stupid and so trivial that even the police can understand that I am breaking the law, you can never touch me!'

He waited for some comment here, but Jim was content to let his host do most of the talking. A footman came in at that moment pushing a basket trolley, and, to Jim's surprise, it contained a silver tea-service, in addition to a bottle of whisky, siphon and glasses.

'I never drink,' explained Harlow. 'When I say "never," it would be better if I said "rarely." Tea-drinking is a pernicious habit which I acquired in my early youth.' He lifted the bottle. 'For you—?'

'Tea also,' said Jim, and Mr Harlow inclined his head.

'I thought that was possible,' he said; and when the servant had gone he carried his tea back to the writing-table and sat down.

'You're a very clever young man,' he said abruptly, and Jim showed his teeth in a sceptical smile. 'I could almost wish you would admit your genius. I hate that form of modesty which is expressed in self-depreciation. You're clever. I have watched your career and have interested myself in your beginning. If you were an ordinary police officer I should not bother with you; but you are something different.'

Again he paused, as though he expected a protest, but neither by word nor gesture did Jim Carlton approve or deny his right to this distinction.

'As for me, I am a rich man,' Harlow went on. 'Yet I need the very help you can give to me. You are not well off, Mr Carlton? I believe you have an income of four hundred a year or thereabouts, apart from your salary, and that is very little for one who sooner or later must feel the need of a home of his own, a wife and a family—'

Again he paused suggestively, and this time Jim spoke.

'What do you suggest to remedy this state of affairs?' he asked.

Mr Harlow smiled.

'You are being sarcastic. There is sarcasm in your voice! You feel that you are superior to the question of money. You can afford to laugh at it. But, my friend, money is a very serious thing. I offer you five thousand pounds a year.'

He rose to his feet the better to emphasize the offer, Jim thought.

'And my duties?' he said quietly.

Harlow shrugged his big shoulders; and put his hands deep into his trousers pockets.

'To watch my interests.' He almost snapped the words. 'To employ that clever brain of yours in furthering my cause, in protecting me when I go – joking! I love a joke – a practical joke. To see the right man squirming makes me laugh. Five thousand a year, and all your expenses paid to the utmost limit. You like play-going? I'll show you a play that will set you rolling with joy! What do you say?'

'No,' said Jim simply; 'I'm not keen on jokes.'

'You're not?' Harlow made a little grimace. 'What a pity! There might be a million in it for you. I am not trying to induce you to do something against your principles, but it is a pity.'

It seemed to Jim's sensitive ear that there was genuine regret in Harlow's tone, but he went on quickly:

'I appreciate your standpoint. You have no desire to enter my service. You are, let us say, antipathetic towards me?'

'I prefer my own work,' said Jim.

Harlow's smile was broad and benevolent.

'There remains only one suggestion: I want you to come to the dinner and reception I am giving to the Middle East delegates next Thursday. Regard that as an olive branch!'

Jim smiled.

'I will gladly accept your invitation, Mr Harlow,' he

said; and then, with scarcely a pause: 'Where can I find Marling?'

The words were hardly out of his lips before he cursed himself for his folly. He had not the slightest intention of asking such a fool question, and he could have kicked himself for the stupid impulse which, in one fraction of a second, had thrown out of gear the delicate machinery of investigation.

Not a muscle of Stratford Harlow's face moved.

'Marling?' he repeated. His black brows met in a frown; the pale eyes surveyed the detective blankly. 'Marling?' he said again. 'Now where have I heard that name? You don't mean the fellow who was my tutor? Good God! what a question to ask! I have never heard of him from the day he left for South Africa or somewhere.'

'The Argentine?' suggested Jim.

'Was it the Argentine? I'm not sure. Yes, I am – Pernambuco – cholera – he died there!'

The underlip came thrusting out. Harlow was passing to the aggressive.

'The truth is, Marling and I were not very good friends. He treated me rather as though I were a child, and I cannot think of him without resentment. Marling! How that word brings back the most uncomfortable memories! The succession of wretched cottages, of prim, neat gardens, of his abominable Greek and Latin verses – differential calculi, the whole horrible gauntlet of so-called education through which a timid youth must run – and be flayed. Why do you ask?'

Jim had his excuse all ready. He might not recover the ground he had lost, but he could at least consolidate himself against further retirement.

'I have had an inquiry from one of his former associates.' He mentioned a name, and here he was on safe ground, for it was the name of a man who had been a contemporary of Marling's and who was in the same college. Not a difficult achievement for Jim, who had spent that morning looking up old university lists. Evidently it had no significance for Harlow.

'I seem to remember Marling talking about him,' he said. 'But twenty-odd years is a very long time to cast back one's memory! And very probably I am an unconscious liar! So far as I know' – he shook his head – 'Marling is dead. I have no absolute proof of this, but if you wish I will have inquiries made. The Argentine Government will do almost anything I wish.'

'You're a lucky man.' Jim held out his hand with a laugh.

'I wonder if I am?' Harlow looked at him steadfastly. 'I wonder! And I wonder if you are, Mr Carlton,' he added slowly. 'Or will be!'

Jim Carlton was not in a position to supply an answer.

His foot was on the doorstep when Harlow called him back.

'I owe you an apology,' he said.

Jim supposed that he was talking about the offer he had made, but this was not the case.

'It was a crude and degrading business, Mr Carlton – but I have a passion for experiment. Such methods were efficacious in the days of our forefathers, and I argued that human nature has not greatly changed.'

Carlton was listening in bewilderment.

'I don't quite follow you—'

Mr Harlow showed his teeth in a smile and for a moment his pale eyes lit up with glee.

'This was not a case of your following me – but of my following you. A crude business. I am heartily ashamed of myself!'

Jim was half-way to Scotland Yard before the solution of this mysterious apology occurred to him. Stratford Harlow was expressing his regret for the attack that had been delivered by his agents in Long Acre.

Jim stopped to scratch his head.

'That man worries me!' he said aloud.

15

THE NEWS that Mr Stratford Harlow was entertaining the Middle East delegates at his house in Park Lane was not of such vital importance that it deserved any great attention from the London press. A three-line paragraph at the foot of a column confirmed the date and the hour. For Jim this proved to be unnecessary, since a reminder came by the second post on the following day, requesting the pleasure of his company at the reception.

'They might have asked me to the dinner,' said Elk. 'Especially as it's free. I'll bet that bird keeps a good brand of cigar.'

'Write and ask for a box; you'll get it,' said Jim, and Elk sniffed.

'That'd be against the best interests of the service,' he said virtuously. 'Do you think I'd get em' if I mentioned your name?'

'You'd get the whole Havana crop,' said Jim. 'I've got a pick. Anyway, there'll be plenty of cigars for you on the night of the reception.'

'Me?' Elk brightened visibly. 'He didn't send me an invite.'

'Nevertheless you are going,' said Jim definitely. 'I'm anxious to know just what this reception is all about. I suppose it's a wonderful thing to stop these brigands from shooting at one another, but I can't see the excuse for a full-scale London party.'

'Maybe he's got a girl he wants to show off,' suggested Elk helpfully.

'You've got a deplorable mind,' was Jim's only comment.

He was not the only hard-worked man in London that week. Every night he walked with Elk and stood opposite the new Rata building in Moorgate Street. Each room was brilliantly illuminated; messengers came and went; and he learnt from one of the extra staff whom he had put into the building, that even Ellenbury, who usually did not allow himself to be identified publicly with the business, was working till three o'clock every morning.

Scotland Yard has many agencies throughout the world, and from these the full extent of Rata's activities began dimly to be seen.

'They've sold nothing, but they're going to sell', reported Jim to his chief at the Yard; 'and it's going to be the biggest bear movement that we have seen in our generation.'

His chief was a natural enemy to the superlatives of youth.

'If it were an offence to "bear" the market I should have no neighbours,' he said icily. 'Almost every stockbroker I know has taken a flutter at some time or other. My information is that the market is firm and healthy. If Harlow is really behind this coup, then he looks like losing money. Why don't you see him and ask him plainly what is the big idea?'

Jim made a face.

'I shall see him tonight at the party,' he said, 'but I doubt very much whether I shall have a chance of worming my way into his confidence!'

Elk was not a society man. It was his dismal claim that not in any rank of the Metropolitan Police Force was there a man with less education than himself. Year after year, with painful regularity, he had failed to pass the examination which was necessary for promotion to the rank of inspector. History floored him; dates of royal accessions and expedient assassinations drove him to despair. Sheer merit eventually secured him the rank which his lack of book learning denied him.

'How'll I do?'

He had come up to Jim's room arrayed for the reception, and now he turned solemnly on his feet to reveal the unusual splendour of evening dress. The tail coat was creased, the trousers had been treated by an amateur cleaner, for they reeked of petrol, and the shirt was soft and yellow with age.

'It's the white weskit that worries me,' he complained. 'They tell me you only wear white weskits for weddin's. But I'm sure the party's goin' to be a fancy one. You wearin' a white weskit?'

'I shall probably wear one,' said Jim soothingly. 'And you look a peach, Elk!'

'They'll take me for a waiter, but I'm used to that,' said Elk. 'Last time I went to a party they made me serve the drinks. Quite a lot never got by!'

'I want you to fix a place where I can find you,' said Jim, struggling with his tail coat. 'That may be very necessary.'

'The bar,' said Elk laconically. 'If it's called a buf-fit, then I'll be at the buf-fit!'

There was a small crowd gathered before the door of Harlow's house. They left a clear lane to the striped awning beneath which the guests passed into the flower-decked vestibule. For the first time Jim saw the millionaire's full domestic staff. A man took his card and did not question the presence of Elk, who strolled nonchalantly past the guardian.

'White weskits!' he hissed. 'I knew it would be fancy!'

The wide doors of the library were thrown open and here Mr Harlow was receiving his guests. Dinner was over and the privileged guests were standing in a half-circle about him.

'White weskit,' murmured Elk, 'and the bar's in the corner of the room.'

Harlow had already seen them; and although Mr Elk was an uninvited guest, he greeted him with warmth. To his companion he gave a warm and hearty hand.

'Have you seen Sir Joseph?' he asked.

Jim had seen the Foreign Secretary that afternoon to learn whether he had made any fresh plans, but had found that Sir Joseph was adhering to his original intention of attending the reception only. He was telling Harlow this when there was a stir at the door and, looking around, he saw the Foreign Secretary enter the room and stop to shake hands with a friend at the door. He wore his black velvet jacket, his long black tie straggled artistically over his white shirt front. Sir Joseph had been pilloried as the worst-dressed man in London and yet, for all his slovenliness of attire, he had the distinctive air of a grand gentleman.

He fixed his horn-rims and favoured Jim with a friendly smile as he made his way to his host.

'I was afraid I could not come,' he said in his husky voice. 'The truth is, some foolish newspaper had been giving prominence to a ridiculous story that went the rounds a few weeks ago; and I had to be in my place to answer a question.'

'Rather late for question time, Sir Joseph,' smiled Harlow. 'I always thought they were taken before the real business of Parliament began.'

Sir Joseph nodded in his jerky way.

'Yes, yes,' he said, a little testily, 'but when questions of policy arise, and a member gives me private notice of his intention of asking such a question, it can be put at any period.'

He swept Parliament and vexatious questioners out of existence with a gesture of his hand.

Jim watched the two men talking together. They were in a deep and earnest conversation, and he gathered from Sir Joseph's gesticulations that the Minister was feeling very strongly on the subject under discussion. Presently they strolled through the crowded library into the vestibule, and after a decent interval Jim went on their trail. He signalled his companion from the buffet and Mr Elk, wiping his moustache hurriedly, joined him as he reached the door.

The guests were still arriving; the vestibule was crowded and progress was slow. Presently a side door in the hall opened, and over the heads of the crush he saw Sir Joseph and Mr Harlow come out and make for the street. Harlow turned back and met the detectives.

'A short visit,' he said, 'but worth while!'

Jim reached the steps in time to see the Foreign Minister's car moving into Park Lane and he had a glimpse of Sir Joseph as he waved his hand in farewell. ...

'He stayed long enough to justify a paragraph in the

morning newspaper – and the uncharitable will believe that that was all I wanted! You're not going?'

It was Harlow speaking.

'I'm sorry, I also have an engagement – in the House!' said Jim good-humouredly; and Mr Harlow laughed.

'I see. You were here on duty as well, eh? Well, that's a very wise precaution. I now realise that not only are you a lucky but you are a short-sighted young man!'

'Why?' asked Jim, so sharply that Harlow laughed.

'I will tell you one of these days,' he said.

The two detectives waited until a taxicab had been hailed; they drove into Palace Yard at the moment Sir Joseph's car was moving back to the rank.

'I don't see why you pulled me away from that party, Carlton,' grumbled Elk. 'Look on this picture and look on that! Look at gay Park Lane and dirty old Westminster!' And then, when his companion did not reply, he asked anxiously: 'Something wrong?'

'I don't know. I've only a sort of feeling that we're going to see an earthquake – that's all,' said Jim emphatically, as they passed into the lobby.

Sir Joseph was in his room and could not be disturbed, a messenger told them. Jim had signed tickets and they passed into the chamber and took a seat under the gallery.

The house was well filled, except the Government benches, which save for the presence of an under-secretary deeply immersed in the contents of his dispatch box, were untenanted. Evidently some motion had been put to the House and the result announced just before the two visitors arrived, for the clerk was reading the terms of an interminable amendment to a Water and Power Bill when Sir Joseph strode in from behind the Speaker's chair, dropped heavily on the bench and, putting on his glasses began to read a sheaf of notes which he carried.

At that moment somebody rose on the Opposition front bench.

'Mr Speaker, I rise to ask the right honourable gentleman a question of which I have given him private notice. The question is: Has the right honourable gentl .man seen a statement published in the *Daily Megaphone* to the effect that relationships between His Majesty's Government and the Government of France are strained as the result of the Bonn incident? And will he tell the House whether such a statement was issued, as is hinted in the newspaper account, with the knowledge and approval of the Foreign Office?'

Sir Joseph rose slowly to his feet, took off his horn-rims and replaced them again, nervously gripped the lapels of his coat, and leaning forward over the dispatch box, spoke:

'The right honourable gentleman is rightly informed,' he began, and a hush fell on the House.

Members looked at one another in amazement and consternation.

'There does exist between His Britannic Majesty's Government and the Government of France a tension which I can only describe as serious. So serious, in fact, that I have felt it necessary to advise the Prime Minister that a state of emergency be declared, all Christmas leave for the Armed Forces be cancelled and that all reserves shall be immediately mobilised.'

A moment of deadly silence. Then a roar of protest. There was hurled at the Government benches a hurricane of indignant questions. Presently the Speaker secured silence; and Sir Joseph went on, in his grave, husky tone:

'I am not prepared to answer any further questions tonight, and I must ask honourable members to defer their judgement until Monday, when I hope to make a statement on behalf of His Majesty's Government.'

And with that, unheeding the calls, he turned and walked behind the Speaker's chair and out of sight.

'Good God!'

Jim was white to the lips.

'That means war!'

Elk, who had fallen into a doze, woke with a start, in time to see his companion dashing out of the House. He followed him along the corridor to Sir Joseph's room and knocked at the door. There was no answer. Jim turned the handle and walked in.

The room was in darkness and empty. Rushing out into the passage, he waylaid a messenger.

'No, sir, I've not seen Sir Joseph. He went into the House a few minutes ago.'

By the time he got back Jim found the lobby crowded with excited members. The Prime Minister was in the West of England; the First Lord of the Admiralty and the Secretary for War had left that afternoon to address a series of public meetings in the North; and already the telephones were busy seeking the other members of the Cabinet. He found nobody who had seen Sir Joseph after he left the House, until he came upon a policeman who thought he had recognised the Foreign Minister walking out into Palace Yard. Jim followed this clue and had it confirmed. Sir Joseph had come out into the Yard and taken a taxi (though his car was waiting), a few minutes before. The detectives almost ran to Whitehall Gardens; and here they had a further shock. The Minister had not arrived at his home.

'Are you sure?' asked Jim incredulously, thinking the butler had orders to rebuff all callers.

'Positive, sir. Why, is anything the matter?' asked the man in alarm.

Jim did not wait to reply. They found a cab in Whitehall and went beyond legal speed to Park Lane. There was just a chance that the Foreign Minister had returned to Harlow's. When they reached Greenhart House there came to them the strains of an orchestra; dancing was in full swing, both in the library and in the large drawing-room overlooking Park Lane. They found Harlow, after a search, and he seemed the most astonished man of all.

'Of course he hasn't come back here. He told me he was going to the House and then home to bed. What has happened?'

'You'll see it in the newspapers in the morning,' said Jim

curtly and drove back to Parliament in time to find the members streaming out of the House, which had been adjourned.

Whilst he was talking with a member he knew, a car drove up and the man who alighted was instantly hailed. It was the Chancellor of the Exchequer, a broad-shouldered man, with a stoop, the most brilliant member of the Cabinet.

'Yes, I've heard all about it,' he said, in his thin, rasping voice. 'Where is Sir Joseph?'

He beckoned Jim, who was known to him and, pushing his way through the crowd of members, went back with him along the corridor to his room.

'Were you in the House when Sir Joseph spoke?' he asked.

'Yes, sir,' said Jim.

'Just tell me what happened.'

Briefly, almost word for word, Jim Carlton repeated the astonishing speech.

'He must be mad,' said the Chancellor emphatically. 'There is not a word of truth in the whole story, unless – well, something may have happened since I saw him last.'

'Can't you issue a denial?'

Mr Kirknoll bit his lip.

'In the absence of the Prime Minister, I suppose I should, but I can't do that until I have seen Sir Joseph.'

A thought struck Jim.

'He is not what one would describe as a neurotic man, is he?'

'No man less so,' said the Chancellor emphatically. 'He is the sanest person I've ever met. Is his secretary in the House?'

He rang a bell and sent a messenger in search, whilst he endeavoured to telephone the absent Ministers.

The secretariat of Downing Street were evidently engaged in a similar quest, with the result that until one in the morning neither had managed to communicate with the head of the Government.

'We can't stop this getting into the newspapers, I suppose?'

'It is in,' said the Chancellor laconically. 'I've just had a copy of the first editions. Why he did it, heaven only knows! He has certainly smashed the Government. What other result will follow I dare not think about.'

'What do you think will be the first result of Sir Joseph's speech?'

The Minister spread out his hands.

'The markets of course will go to blazes, but that doesn't interest us so much as the feeling it may create in France. Unhappily, the French Ambassador is in Paris on a short visit.'

Jim left him talking volubly on the Paris line and at three o'clock in the morning was reading a verbatim report of Sir Joseph Layton's remarkable lapse. The later editions carried eight lines in heavy type:

> **We are informed by the Chancellor of the Exchequer that the Bonn incident has never been before the Cabinet for discussion, and it is not regarded as being of the slightest importance. The Chancellor informs us that he cannot account for Sir Joseph Layton's extraordinary statement in the House of Commons.**

All night long Jim literally sat on the doorstep of Whitehall Gardens, waiting without any great hope for Sir Joseph's return. He learnt that the Prime Minister was returning from the West by special train; and that a statement had already been issued repudiating that of the Foreign Minister.

The opening of the Stock Exchange that morning was witnessed by scenes which had no parallel since the outbreak of the War. Stocks declined to an incredible extent, and even the banks reacted to the panic. It was too early to learn what had happened in New York, the British being five hours in advance of Eastern American time, and only at four o'clock that afternoon was the position on Wall Street revealed. Heavy selling – all gilt-edged stocks depreciated; the failure of a big broking house, were the first consequences observable in the press. In France the Bourse had been closed at noon, but there was heavy street selling; and one famous South African stock, which was the barometer in the market, had dropped to its lowest level.

At five o'clock that evening a statement was issued to the press over the signatures of the Prime Ministers of Britain and France.

There is no truth whatever in the statement that a state of tension exists between our two countries. The Bonn incident has been from first to last regarded as trivial, and the speech of the British Foreign Minister can only have been made in a moment of regrettable mental aberration.

For Jim the day's interest had nothing whatever to do with stock exchanges or the fall of shares; nor yet the fortune which he knew was being gathered, with every minute that passed, by Harlow and his agents. His interest was solely devoted to the mystery of Sir Joseph Layton's disappearance.

There had been present at Harlow's reception a very large number of notable people, many of whom were personal friends of the missing Minister. They were emphatic in declaring that he had not returned to Park Lane; and they were as certain that Harlow had not left the house after Sir Joseph's departure. More than this, there were two policemen on duty at the door; and they were equally certain that Sir Joseph had not returned. The suggestion was made that the Minister had gone to his country house in Cheshire, but when inquiry was set on foot it was learned that the house and the shooting had been rented by a rich American.

Immediately he had returned to London the Prime Minister flew to Paris. When he got back Jim saw him, and the chief officer of state was a greatly worried as well as a very tired man.

'Sir Joseph Layton has to be found!' he said, thumping his table. 'I tell you this, Carlton, as I have told your superiors, that it was impossible, unless Sir Joseph went mad, that he could have stood up in the House of Commons and said something which he knew to be absolutely untrue, and which he himself would repudiate! Have you seen this man Harlow?'

'Yes, sir,' said Jim.

'Did he tell you what was discussed by any chance? Was it the so-called Bonn incident?'

'Harlow says that they just talked about the Middle East and nothing else during the few minutes the Foreign Minister was in his house. And really, sir, I don't see how they could have had any very lengthy discussion; they were not together more than a few minutes. Apparently Sir Joseph went into a little room which Harlow uses for his more confidential interviews and drank a glass of wine. They then talked about the reception and Sir Joseph congratulated him on bringing the warring elements together. It seems to have been, according to Harlow's account, the most uninteresting talk.'

The Prime Minister walked up and down the room with long strides, his chin on his chest.

'I can't understand it, I can't understand it!' he muttered. And then, abruptly: 'Find Sir Joseph Layton.'

That terminated the interview for Jim.

He was rattled, badly rattled, and in his distraction he could think of only one sedative. He rang up Aileen Rivers at her office and asked her to come to tea with him at the Automobile Club.

Aileen realised from the first that Jim was directly occupied by a mystery that was puzzling not only the country but the whole of the civilised world. But she understood also the reason he had sent for her, and the thought that she was being of use to him was a very pleasant one.

As soon as he met her he plunged straight into the story of his trouble.

'He may have been kidnapped, of course, and I should say it was very likely, though the distance between Palace Yard and Whitehall Gardens is very short; and Whitehall is so full of police that it hardly seems possible. We have advertised for the taximan who drove him away from the House, but so far have had no reply.'

'Perhaps the taximan was also kidnapped?' she suggested.

'Perhaps so,' he admitted. 'I do wish Foreign Ministers weren't so godlike that they have to travel alone! If he'd only waited a few minutes I would have joined him.' And then, with a smile: 'I'm laying my burdens upon you and you're wilting visibly.'

'I'm not,' she affirmed.

She considered a moment before she asked:

'Could I not help you?'

He stared at her in amused wonder.

'How on earth could you help me? I'm being rude I know, but I can't exactly see—'

She was annoyed rather than hurt by his scepticism.

'It may be a very presumptuous thing to offer assistance to the police,' she said with a faint hint of sarcasm, 'but I think what may be wrong with you now is that you want – what is the expression? – a new angle?'

'I certainly want several new angles,' he confessed ruefully.

'Then I'll start in to give you one. Have you seen my uncle?'

His jaw dropped. He had forgotten all about Arthur Ingle; and never once had he associated him with the Minister's disappearance.

'What a fool I am!' he gasped.

She examined his face steadily, as though she were considering whether or not to agree. In reality her mind was very far away.

'I only suggest my uncle because he called upon me this morning,' she said. 'At least, he was waiting for me when I came out to lunch. It is the first time I have seen him since the night he came back from Devonshire.'

'What did he want to see you about?'

She laughed softly.

'He came with a most extraordinary offer, that I should keep house for him. And really, he offered me considerably more than the salary I am getting from Stebbings, and said he had no objection to my working in the daytime.'

'You refused, of course?'

'I refused, of course,' she repeated, 'but he wasn't at all put out. I've never seen him in such an amiable frame of mind.'

'How does he look?' asked Jim, remembering the unshaven face he had seen through the window.

'Very smart,' was the surprising reply. 'He told me he had been amusing himself with some of the big films that had appeared since he went to prison. He had hired them and bought a small projector. He really was fond of the pictures, as I know,' the girl went on, 'but it seems a queer thing to have shut oneself up for days just to watch films! And he asked after you.' She nodded. 'Why should he ask after you, you are going to say, and that is the question that occurred to me. But he seems to have taken for granted that I am a very close friend of yours. He asked who had introduced me, and I told him your wretched little car on the Thames Embankment!'

'Speak well of the dead,' said Jim soberly. 'Lizzie has cracked a cylinder.'

'And now,' she said, 'prepare for a great shock.'

'I brace myself,' said Jim.

'He asked,' the girl went on, a twinkle in her eyes, 'whether I thought you would object to seeing him. I think he must have taken a sudden liking to you.'

'I've never met the gentleman,' said Jim, 'but that is an omission which shall be rectified without delay. We'll go round together! He will naturally jump at the conclusion that we're an engaged couple, but if you can stand that slur on your intelligence—'

'I will be brave,' said Aileen.

Mr Arthur Ingle was only momentarily disconcerted by the appearance of his niece and the man who had filled his mind all that afternoon. Jim had met him once before, but only for a few seconds, when he had called to make an inquiry about Mrs Gibbins. Now he was almost jovial.

'Where's friend Elk?' he asked, with a smile. 'I understood you never moved without one another in these perilous times, when lunatic ministers are wandering about the country, and no man knows the hour or the day when he will be called up for active service! So you are Mr James Carlton!'

He opened a silver cigar-box and pushed it across to Jim, who made a careful selection.

'Aileen told you I wanted to see you, I suppose? Well, I do. I'm a bit of a theorist, Mr Carlton, and I have an idea that my theory is right. I wonder if you would be interested to know what it is?'

He pointedly ignored the presence of the girl except to put a chair for her.

'I've been making inquiries,' said this surprising ex-convict, 'and I've discovered that Sir Joseph is in all sorts of financial difficulties. This is unknown to the Prime Minister or even to his closest friend, but I have had a hint that he was very short of ready money and that his estates in Cheshire were heavily mortgaged. Now, Mr Carlton, do you conceive it as possible that the speech in the House was made with the deliberate intention of slumping the market and that Sir Joseph was paid handsomely for the part he played?'

As he was speaking, he clasped his hands before him, his fingers intertwined; he emphasised every point with a little jerk of his clasped hands and, watching him, the mist rolled from Jim Carlton's brain, and he instantly solved the mystery of those private film shows which had kept Mr Ingle locked up in his flat for a week. And to solve that was to solve every mystery save the present whereabouts of Sir Joseph Layton.

He listened in silence whilst Ingle went on to expound and elaborate his theory and when the man had finished:

'I will bring your suggestion to the notice of my superiors,' he said conventionally.

It was evidently not the speech that Mr Ingle expected. For a moment he looked uncomfortable, and then, with a laugh:

'I suppose you think it strange that I should be on the

side of law and order – and the governing classes! I felt a little sore when I came out of prison. Elk probably told you of the exhibition I made of myself in the train. But I've been thinking things over, Carlton, and it has occurred to me that my extremism is not profitable either to my pocket or my mind.'

'In fact,' smiled Jim, 'you're going to become a reformed character and a member of the good old Tory party?'

'I don't know that I shall go as far as that,' demurred the other, amused, 'but I have decided to settle down. I am not exactly a poor man, and all that I have got I have paid for – in Dartmoor.'

Only for a second were the old harsh cadences audible in his voice. He nodded towards Aileen Rivers.

'You'll persuade this girl to give me a chance, Mr Carlton? I can well understand her hesitation to keep house for a man liable at any moment to be whisked off to durance, and I fear she does not quite believe in my reformation.'

He smiled blandly at the girl, and then turned his eyes upon Jim.

'Could you not persuade her?'

'If I could persuade her to any course,' said Jim deliberately, 'it would not be the one you suggest.'

'Why?' challenged the other.

'Because,' said Jim, 'you are altogether wrong when you say that there is no longer any danger of your being whisked off to durance. The danger was never more pressing.'

Ingle did not reply to this. Once his lips trembled as though he were about to ask a question, and then with a laugh he walked to the table and took a cigar from the box.

'I guess I won't detain you,' he said. 'But you're wrong, Carlton. The police have nothing on me! They may frame something to catch me, but you'll have to be clever to do even that.'

As they passed out of the building:

'I seem to spend my days giving warnings to the last people in the world who ought to be warned,' said Jim bitterly. 'Aileen, maybe you'll knit me a muzzle in your spare moments? That will help considerably!'

The outstanding feature of this little speech from the girl's point of view was that he had called her by her name for the first time. Later, when they were nearing her boarding house, she asked:

'Do you think you will find Sir Joseph?'

He shook his head.

'I doubt very much if he is alive,' he said gravely.

But his doubts were to be dispelled, and in the most surprising manner. That night a drunken black-faced comedian hit a policeman over the head with a banjo, and that vulgar incident had an amazing sequel.

16

THERE IS a class of entertainer which devotes its talents to amusing the queues that wait at the doors of the cheaper entrances of London's theatres. Here is generally to be found a man who can tear paper into fantastic shapes, a ballad singer or two, a performer on the bones and the inevitable black-faced minstrel.

It was eleven o'clock at night, and snow was lightly falling, when a policeman on point duty at the end of Evory Street saw a figure staggering along the middle of the road, in imminent danger from the returning theatre traffic. The man had obviously taken more drink than was good for him, for he was howling at the top of his voice the song of the moment; and making a clumsy attempt to accompany himself on the banjo which was slung around his neck.

The London police are patient and long-suffering people, and had the reeling figure been less vocal he might have passed on to his destination without interference. For drunkenness in itself is not a crime according to the law; a man must be incapable or create a disturbance, or obstruct the police in the execution of their duty, before he offends. The policeman had no intention of arresting the noisy wayfarer. He walked into the middle of the road to intercept and quieten him; and then discovered that the reveller was a black-faced comedian with extravagant white lips, a ridiculous Eton collar and a shell coat. On his head was a college cap, and this completed his outfit with the exception of the banjo, with which he was making horrid sounds.

'Hi, hi!' said the policeman gently. 'A little less noise, young fellow!'

Such an admonition would have been sufficient in most cases to have reduced a midnight song-bird to apology, but this street waif stood defiantly in the middle of the road, his legs apart, and invited the officer to go to a warmer climate, and, not satisfied with this, he swung his banjo, and brought it down with a crash on the policeman's helmet.

'You've asked for it!' said the officer of the law and took his lawful prey in a grip of iron.

By a coincidence, Jim Carlton was at Evory Street Station when the man was brought in, singing not unmusically, and so obviously drunk that Jim hardly turned his head or interrupted the conversation he was having with the inspector on duty, to look at the charge. They made a rapid search of the man, he resisting violently and at last, when they had extracted a name (he refused his address) he was hustled between a policeman and a jailer into the long corridor off which the cells are placed.

The door of Cell No. 7 was opened and into this he was pushed, struggling to the last to maintain his banjo.

'And,' said the jailer when he came back to the charge-room, wiping his perspiring brow, 'the language that bird is using would turn a soldier pale!'

The reason for Jim's presence was to arrange a local supervision of Greenhart House and to obtain certain assistance in the execution of a plan which was running through his mind; and that task would have been completed when the black-faced man was brought in, but that the officer he had called to see was away. Jim lingered a little while, talking police shop, before he paid his last visit to Sir Joseph's house. He had the inevitable reply: No News had reached Whitehall Gardens of the Foreign Minister.

The man he came to see at Evory Street was due to appear at the police court in the rôle of prosecutor and Jim strolled down to the court next morning, arriving soon after the magistrate had taken his seat. There he met the inspector from Evory Street. Before Jim could broach the subject which had brought him, the inspector asked:

'Were you at the station when that black-faced fellow was pulled in last night?'

'Yes, I remember the noisy gentleman,' said Jim. 'Why?'

The inspector shook his head, puzzled.

'I can't understand where he got it from. The sergeant searched him carefully, but he must have had it concealed in some place.'

'What is the matter with him?' asked Jim, only half interested.

'Dope,' said the other. 'When the jailer went and called him this morning it was as much as he could do to wake him up. In fact, he thought of sending for the divisional surgeon. You never saw a sicker-looking man in your life! Can't get a word out of him. All he did was to sit on his bed with his head in his hands, moaning. We had to shake him to get him into the prison van.'

The first two cases were disposed of rapidly, and then a policeman called: 'John Smith,' and there tottered into court the black-faced comedian, a miserable object, so weak of knee that he had to be guided up the steps into the steel-railed dock. Gone was the exhilaration of the night before, and Jim had an unusual feeling of pity for the poor wretch in his absurd clothes and black, shining face.

The magistrate looked over his glasses.

'Why wasn't this man allowed to wash his face before he came before me?' he asked.

'Couldn't get him to do anything, sir,' said the jailer, 'and we haven't got the stuff to take off this make-up.'

The magistrate grumbled something, and the assaulted policeman stepped into the box and took his oath to tell the truth and nothing but the truth. He gave his stereotyped evidence and again the magistrate looked at the drooping figure in the dock.

'What have you to say, Smith?' he asked.

The man did not raise his head.

'Is anything known about him? I notice that his address is not on the charge sheet.'

'He refused his address, your Worship,' said the inspector.

'Remanded for inquiries!'

The jailer touched the prisoner's arm and he looked up at him suddenly; stared wildly round the court, and then:

'May I ask what I am doing here?' he asked in a husky voice, and Jim's jaw dropped.

For the black-faced man was Sir Joseph Layton!

17

EVEN THE magistrate was startled, though he did not recognise the voice. He was about to give an order for the removal of the man when Jim pushed his way to his desk and whispered a few words.

'Who?' asked the magistrate. 'Impossible!'

'May I ask' – it was the prisoner speaking again – 'what is all this about – I really do not understand.'

And then he swayed and would have fallen, but the jailer caught him in his arms.

'Take him out into my room.' The magistrate was on his feet. 'The court stands adjourned for ten minutes,' he said; and disappeared behind the curtains into his office.

A few seconds later they brought in the limp figure of the prisoner and laid him on a sofa.

'Are you sure? You must be mistaken, Mr Carlton!'

'I am perfectly sure – even though his moustache has been shaved off,' said Jim, looking into the face of the unconscious man. 'This is Sir Joseph Layton, the Foreign Minister. I could not make a mistake. I know him so well.'

The magistrate peered closer.

'I almost think you are right,' he said, 'but how on earth—'

He did not complete his sentence; and soon after he went out to carry on the business of the court. Jim had sent an officer to a neighbouring chemist for a pot of cold cream; and by the time the divisional surgeon arrived all doubt as to the identity of the black-faced man had been removed with his make-up. His white hair was stained, his moustache removed, and so far as they could see, not one stitch of his clothing bore any mark which would have identified him.

The doctor pulled up the sleeve and examined the forearm.

'He has been doped very considerably,' he said, pointing to a number of small punctures. 'I don't exactly know what drug was used, but there was hyoscin in it, I'll swear.'

Leaving Sir Joseph to the care of the surgeon, Jim hurried out to the telephone and in a few minutes was in communication with the Prime Minister.

'I'll come along in a few minutes,' said that astonished gentleman. 'Be careful that nothing about this gets into the papers – will you please ask the magistrate, as a special favour to me, to make no reference in court?'

Fortunately, only one police-court reporter had been present, he had seen nothing that aroused his suspicion and his curiosity as to why the prisoner had been carried to the magistrate's room was easily satisfied.

Sir Joseph was still unconscious when the Premier arrived. An ambulance had been summoned and was already in the little courtyard, and after a vain attempt to get him to speak, the Foreign Secretary was smuggled out into the yard, wrapped in a blanket and dispatched to a nursing home.

'I confess I'm floored,' said the Prime Minister in despair. 'A nigger minstrel ... assaulting the police! It is incredible! You say you were at the police station when he was brought in; didn't you recognise him then?'

'No, sir,' said Jim truthfully, 'I was not greatly interested – he seemed just an ordinary drunk to me. But one thing I will swear; he was not under the influence of any drug when he was brought into the station. The inspector said he reeked of whisky, and he certainly found no difficulty in giving expression to his mind!'

The Premier threw out despairing hands.

'It is beyond me; I cannot understand what has happened. The whole thing is monstrously incredible. I feel I must be dreaming.'

As soon as the Premier had gone, Jim drove to the nursing home to which the unfortunate Minister had been taken. The Evory Street inspector had gone with the ambulance, and had an astonishing story to tell.

'What do you think we found in his pocket?' he asked.

'You can't startle me,' said Jim recklessly. 'What was it – the Treaty of Versailles?'

The inspector opened his pocket-book and took out a small blank visiting card, blank, that is, except for a number of scratches, probably made by some blunt instrument, but the writer had attempted to get too much on so small a space, for Jim saw that it was writing when he examined the card carefully. Two words were decipherable, 'Marling' and 'Harlow' and these had been printed in capitals. He took a lead pencil, scraped the point upon the card, and sifted the fine dust over the scratches until they became more definite. The writing was still indecipherable even with such an aid to legibility as the lead powder. Apparently the message had been written with a pin, for in two places the card was perforated.

'The first word is "whosoever", ' said Jim suddenly. ' "Whosoever ... please" is the fourth word and that seems to be underlined ...'

He studied the card for a long time and then shook his head.

' "Harlow" is clear and "Marling" is clear. What do you make of it, inspector?'

The officer took the card from his hand and examined it with a blank expression.

'I don't know anything about the writing or what it means,' he said. 'The thing I am trying to work out is how did that card come in his pocket – it was not there last night when the sergeant searched him – he takes his oath on it!'

18

A BRIEF paragraph appeared in the morning newspapers.

Sir Joseph Layton, Secretary of State for Foreign Affairs, is seriously ill in a nursing home.

It would take more than this simple paragraph to restore the markets of the world to the level they had been when the threat of war had sent them tumbling like a house of cards. The principal item of news remained this world panic, which the Foreign Secretary's speech had initiated. A great economist computed that the depreciation in gilt-edged securities represented over £100,000,000 sterling and whilst the downward tendency at least to some stocks was recovering, a month or more must pass before the majority reached the pre-scare level. One newspaper, innocent of the suspicion under which the financier lay in certain quarters, interviewed Mr Harlow.

'I think,' said Mr Stratford Harlow, 'that the effect of the slump has been greatly exaggerated. In many ways, such a panic has ultimately a beneficial result. It finds out all the feeble spots in the structure of finance, breaks down the weak links, so that in the end the fabric is stronger and more wholesome than it was before the slump occurred.'

'Is it possible that the slump was engineered by a group of market-riggers?'

Mr Harlow scoffed at the idea.

'How could it have been engineered without the connivance or assistance of the Foreign Secretary, whose speech alone was responsible?' he asked. 'It is certainly an amazing statement for a responsible Minister to make. Apparently Sir John was a very sick man when he addressed the House of Commons. It is suggested that he was suffering from overwork, but whatever may have been the cause, he, and he alone, brought about this slump,'

'You knew Sir John?'

Mr Harlow agreed.

'He was in my house, in this very room, less than a quarter of an hour before the speech was made,' he said, 'and I can only say that he appeared in every way normal. If he was ill, he certainly did not show it.'

Reverting to the question of world-wide depreciation of stock values, Mr Harlow went on to say ...

Jim read the interview with a wry smile. Harlow had said many things, but he had omitted many more. He did not speak of the feverish activity of Rata, Limited, whose every window had been blazing throughout a week of nights – not one word had he suggested that he himself would benefit to an enormous extent through the tragedy of that unhappy speech.

The man puzzled him. If he was, as Jim was convinced, behind the scare, if his clever brain had devised, and by some mysterious means had brought about the financial panic, what end had he in view? He had been already one of the three richest men in England. He had not the excuse that he had a mammoth industry to benefit. He had no imperial project to bring to fruition. Had he been dreaming of new empires created out of the wilds; were he a great philanthropist who had some gigantic enterprise to advance for the benefit of mankind, this passionate desire for gold might be understood if it could not be excused.

But Harlow had no other objective than the accumulation of money. He had shown a vicarious interest in the public weal when he had presented his model police station to the country; he had certainly subscribed liberally to hospital appeals; but none of these gifts belonged to a system of charity or public spirit. He was a man without social gifts – the joys or suffering of his fellows struck no sympathetic chord in his nature. If he gave, he gave cold-bloodedly, and yet without ostentation.

True, he had offered to build, on the highest point of the Chiltern Hills, an exact replica of the Parthenon as a national war memorial, but the offer had been rejected because of the inaccessibility of the chosen spot. There was a certain freakishness in his projects; and Jim suspected that they were not wholly disinterested. The man baffled him: he could get no thread that would lead him to the soul and the mind behind those cold blue eyes.

For six hours that night he sat by the bedside of the unconscious Foreign Minister. What strange story could he tell, Jim wondered. How came he to be perambulating the streets in the guise of a drunken mountebank, whose wanderings were to end in a vulgar brawl, with a policeman and the cheerless lodgings of a prison cell? Had he some secret weakness which Harlow had learnt and exploited? Did he live a double life? Jim thought only to reject the idea. Sir Joseph's life was more or less an open book; his movements for years past could be traced day by day from the information supplied by the diaries of his secretary, from the knowledge of his own colleagues.

Whilst Jim kept his vigil he made another attempt to decipher the writing on the card, but he got no farther. He was taking turns with Inspector Wilton of Evory Street in watching beside the bedside. The doctor had said that at any moment the Minister might recover consciousness; and though he took the gravest view of the ultimate result of the drugging, his prognosis did not exclude the chance of a complete recovery. It was at a quarter after three in the morning that the sick man, who had been tossing from side to side, muttering disjointed words which had no meaning to the listener, turned upon his back and, opening his eyes, blinked round the dimly lighted room. Jim, who had been studying the card in the light of a shaded lamp, put it into his pocket and came to the side of the bed.

Sir Joseph looked at him wonderingly, his wide brows knit in an effort of memory.

'Hullo!' he said faintly. 'What happened ... ? Did the car smash up?'

'Nothing serious has happened, Sir Joseph,' said Jim gently.

Again the wondering eyes wandered around the bare walls of the room, and then they fell upon a temperature chart hanging against the wall.

'This is a hospital, isn't it?'

'A nursing home,' said Jim.

There was a long silence before the sick man spoke.

'My head aches infernally. Can you give me a drink, or isn't that allowed?'

Jim poured out a glass of water and, supporting the shoulders of the Minister, put the glass to his lips. He drank the contents greedily and sank back with a sigh upon the pillow.

'I suppose I am a little light-headed, but I could swear that your name was Carlton,' he said.

'That is my name, sir,' said Jim, and the Minister pondered this for a little time.

'Anything broken?' he asked. 'It was the car, I suppose? I told that stupid chauffeur of mine to be careful. The road was like glass.'

He moved first one leg and then the other gingerly, and then his arms.

'Nothing is broken at all, Sir Joseph,' said Jim. 'You have had a shock.'

He had already rung for the doctor, who was sleeping in a room below.

'Shock, eh? ... I don't remember ... And Harlow!' His eyebrows lowered again. 'A decent fellow but rather over-dressed. I went to his house tonight, didn't I ... ? Yes, yes, I remember. How long ago was it?'

Jim would not tell him that the visit to Harlow's had happened days before.

'Yes, yes, I remember now. Where did I go after that ... to the House, I suppose? My mind is like a whirling ball of wool!'

The doctor came in, a dressing-gown over his pyjamas, and the Minister's mind was sufficiently clear to guess his profession.

'I'm all in, doctor. What was it, a stroke?'

'No Sir Joseph,' said the doctor. He was feeling his patient's pulse and seemed satisfied.

'Sir Joseph thinks he might have been in a car collision,' suggested Jim with a significant glance at the doctor.

The man was terribly weak, but the brightness of his intellect was undimmed.

'What is the matter with me?' he asked irritably as the medical man put the stethoscope to his heart.

'I'm wondering whether you have ever taken drugs in your life?'

'Drugs!' snorted the old man. 'Good God! What a question! I don't even take medicine! When I feel ill I go to my osteopath and he puts me right.'

The doctor grinned, as all properly constituted doctors grin when an osteopath is mentioned, for the medical profession is the most conservative and the most suspicious of any.

'Then I shan't give you drugs.' He had a nimble turn of mind to cover up an awkward question. 'Your heart is good and your pulse is good. And all you want now is a little sleep.'

'And a little food,' growled Sir Joseph. 'I am as hungry as a starved weasel!'

They brought him some chicken broth, hot and strong, and in half an hour he had fallen into a gentle sleep. The doctor beckoned Jim outside the room.

'I think it is safe for you to leave him,' he said. 'He is making a better recovery than I dreamt was possible. I suppose he has said nothing about his adventures?'

'Nothing,' said Jim, and the man of medicine realised

140

that, even if Sir Joseph had explained the strange circumstances of his arrest and appearance in the police court, it was very unlikely that he would be told.

Early the next morning Jim called at Downing Street and saw the Prime Minister.

'He is under the impression that he was in a car accident after leaving Park Lane. He remembers nothing about the speech in the House; the doctors will not allow him to be told until he is strong again. I have very grave doubt on one point, sir, which I want to clear up. And to clear it up it may be necessary to go outside the law.'

'I don't care very much where you go,' said the Prime Minister, 'but we must have the truth! Until the facts are known, not only Sir Joseph but the whole Cabinet is under a cloud. I will give instructions that you are to have *carte blanche*, and I will support you in any action you may take.'

With this confident assurance Jim went on to Scotland Yard to prove the truth of a theory which had slowly evolved in the dark hours of the night; a theory so fantastical that he could hardly bring himself to its serious contemplation.

19

FOUR HUNDRED and fifteen cablegrams were put on the wire in one morning and they were all framed in identical terms:

Remit by cable through Lombard Bank Carr Street Branch all profits taken in Rata Transaction 17 to receipt of this instruction. Acknowledge. Rata.

This message was dispatched at three o'clock in the morning from the GPO.

The Foreign Department manager of the Lombard Bank was an old friend of Mr Ellenbury, and had done business with him before. Mr Ellenbury drove to the bank the following afternoon and saw the head of the Foreign Department.

'I am expecting some very extensive cable remittances through the Lombard,' he said, 'and I shall want cash.'

The sour-looking manager looked even more sour.

'Rata's, I suppose? I'm surprised that you are mixed up with these people, Mr Ellenbury. I don't think you can know what folks are saying in the City. ...'

He was a friend and was frank. Mr Ellenbury listened meekly.

'One cannot pick and choose,' he said. 'The war made a great deal of difference to me; I must live.'

The war is an unfailing argument to explain changed conditions and can be employed as well to account for adaptable standards of morality. The manager accepted the other's viewpoint with reservations.

'How much has Harlow made out of this swindle?' he asked, again exercising the privilege of friendship.

'Someday I will tell you,' said the lawyer cryptically. 'The point is, I expect very large sums.'

'Sterling or what?'

'Any currency that is stable,' said Mr Ellenbury.

That evening came the first advice – from Johannesburg. The sum remitted was not colossal, but it was large. New Orleans arrived in the night and was delivered to Mr Ellenbury with Chicago, New York, Toronto and Sydney. The cable advices accumulated; Mr Ellenbury took no steps to draw the money that was piling up at the Lombard Bank until the second day.

On the morning of that day he walked round his bedraggled demesne before going to the City. He had grown attached to Royalton House, he discovered, and almost wished he could take it with him. It was ugly and dreary and depressing. Even the vegetable garden seemed decayed. Pale ghosts of cabbages drooped like aged and mourning men amidst the skeleton stalks of their departed fellows.

Across the desolation came the gardener, his shoulders protected from the drizzle by a sack.

'I've got a load of stuff to fill the pit,' he said. 'Came yesterday.'

The pit was an eyesore and had been for thirty years. It was a deep depression at the edge of the kitchen garden and Mr Ellenbury had sited many dreams upon it. An ornamental pound, surrounded by banked rhododendrons. A swimming pool with a white-tiled bed and marble seats, where, hidden from the vulgar eye by trellised roses, a bather might sit and bask in the sun. Now it was the end of dreams – a pit to be filled. He stood on the edge of it. An unlovely hole in the ground, the bottom covered with water, the rusty corner of a petrol tin showing just above the surface.

By the side was a heap of rubbish, aged bricks and portions of brick, sand gravel, sheer ashpit emptyings.

'I will fill it in – I have promised myself that exercise,' said Mr Ellenbury, forgetting for the moment that by tomorrow he would be filling in nothing more substantial than time.

The slimy hole held his eyes. If he could put Harlow there and see his big white face staring up from the mud – that would be a good filling!

He felt his face and neck go red, his limbs tingling. Presently he tore himself away and walked back to the house. The car that Rata's hired for him was waiting – the driver bade him a civil good morning and said the weather was the worst he had ever known.

Mr Ellenbury went in to breakfast without replying. The sight of the car was suggestive.

There was another garage known to Mr Ellenbury where a car could be hired and no inconvenient questions asked. Stated more clearly, there are many people in London engaged in peculiar professions, to whom money was not an important consideration. They could not buy loyalty, but they were willing to pay for discretion.

Nova's Garage had a tariff that was considerably higher

than any other, but the extra cost was money well spent. For when the police came to Nova's to learn who was the foreign-looking gentleman who had driven away from a West End jeweller's with the diamond ring he had bought and the row of pearls that had disappeared with him, Nova's were blandly ignorant. Nor could they recognise the lady who had driven the rich Bradford merchant to Marlow and left him drugged and penniless in the long grass of the meadows.

In the afternoon the car came; the chauffeur was a burly man with a black moustache who chewed gum and had no interest in anybody's business but his own.

In this Mr Ellenbury drove to the bank, taking his two suitcases; and went into the manager's room and checked the cable advices.

'Immense!' said the manager soberly. He referred to the total. 'And more to come, I suppose? It is so big that it almost breaks loose from the standards.'

'Standards?'

Mr Ellenbury did not know what he was talking about.

'Right and wrong ... like taking a foot-rule to measure St Paul's.'

Ellenbury, something of a dialectician, could not resist the challenge.

'Moral conduct isn't a matter of arithmetic, but a matter of proportion. You can't measure it with a yard-stick, but by its angle. Ten degrees out of the perpendicular is as much a fault in a gate-post as in the leaning Tower of Pisa. ... I make this American total a hundred and twelve thousand.'

'And ten,' added the manager. 'The exchange is against us.'

Mr Ellenbury made five bundles of the notes and fitted them into the suitcase.

'Now we will take the South African remittances,' said the manager, painfully patient, a sigh in his every sentence, disapproval in every wag of his pen. 'I suppose you're right, but it does seem to me that a man's offence against society is in inverse ratio to the amount of money he pouches.'

'Pouches!' murmured Mr Ellenbury in protest.

' "Pockets", then. When you reach the million mark you've got to a point beyond the comprehension of a jury. They look at the man and they look at the money, and they say "not guilty" automatically. There ought to be a new set of laws dealing with property – starting with penalties for pinching a million; and working up to the place where you can indict a government for wasting nine figures. And the jury should be made up of accountants and novelists, who've never seen real money but think in millions – eighty-seven thousand nine hundred I make it.'

Mr Ellenbury performed a rapid calculation, consulting a little ready reckoner.

'Right,' he said. 'You have strangely perverted principles, my friend. Whether a man steals ten cents or five million dollars—'

'Bank of Yokohama' – the manager sorted his papers. 'The yen is at 17/9, that's a drop. Curious! Way down in the bowels of the earth a ledge of rock slips over, a super-heated packet of steam blows up, and the effect on the money market is disastrous! There is a lot of earthquake in Harlow: he has got into the Acts of God class – I'm giving you dollars for this – US dollars.'

'Quite OK,' said Mr Ellenbury, checking the bundles that were handed to him.

It was growing dark when he carried out his suitcases and placed them inside the car. They were very heavy. It was strange how heavy paper money could be – and how bulky.

He drove to his office in Theobald's Road and was glad that many years before, when offered the choice between a small suite on the ground floor and a larger one on the first floor, he had chosen the former.

He had sent his clerk home early. It was a Friday and the man had been given a fortnight's holiday and had had his salary in advance. Opening the outer door with his key, he tugged the two suitcases into his private room. Here was a brand-new trunk and a passport. A few weeks before,

Harlow had ordered him to procure a passport for a 'Mr Jackson,' whose other name was Ingle. Ellenbury had a distaste for the petty frauds of life, but as usual he had obeyed and duplicated the offence by applying for a second passport, forwarding a photograph of himself taken twenty years before and applying in a name which had not the faintest resemblance to his own.

He sat down with the two bulging grips before him and with a feeling of growing unease. Not that his conscience was troubling him. The bedridden Mrs Ellenbury never once entered his mind; the injustice he was doing to his employer, if it occurred to him at all, was a relief to his distress.

The weight and the bulk of the paper money. ...

The Customs would search his suitcase at Calais or Havre, and the money would attract attention. He might put it at the bottom of the trunk and register it through. But the thefts of baggage on the French railways were notoriously frequent. He might, of course, travel by the Simplon Express or by the Blue Train – hand baggage was subject to a perfunctory examination on the train, and if he were bound for Monte Carlo the carriage of such wealth might be regarded as an act of madness by the Customs officials and excite no other comment.

But both the Simplon and the Riviera Express are booked up at this season of the year and a compartment could not be secured by any influence. He might fly but he feared that the Airport scrutiny would be even more severe.

There remained only one alternative. To carry half the money in his trunk, distribute as much as he could amongst his pockets and post the rest to himself at various hotels throughout France and Spain. And this would be a long and tedious job. He went into the outer office and brought back a packet of stout envelopes. He must not register them – these Latin post offices made the collection of a registered letter a fussy business.

20

WITH A Bradshaw by his side, he began his task. He exhausted the envelopes and went in search of another packet, but could find none of the requisite stoutness. Extinguishing the lights, he went out to a neighbouring store, replenished his stock and came back. Halfway through the second packet, with the table piled with bulging envelopes, he was writing:

Hotel Riena Christina,
  Algeciras——

when there was a tap on the green baize door and he nearly screamed with fright.

Two grave eyes were watching him through the oval of glass that gave a view into the office. Leaping to his feet, his teeth set in a grin of fear, he dragged open the door.

A girl stood on the threshold. She wore a long blue coat; there were beads of rain on the shoulders and on the head scarf. In her hand was a streaming umbrella. Mr Ellenbury had not noticed it was raining.

She was staring at the open suitcases, at the bundles of notes, the heaped envelopes. Aileen Rivers had never seen so much money.

'Well!' Ellenbury's voice was a harsh squeak.

'I tried to find your clerk,' she said. 'The door was open—'

Open? In his haste to continue his work Ellenbury had not closed the outer door – had not even shut the door beyond the baize.

He recognized her.

'You're Stebbings's girl,' he said breathlessly. 'What do you want!'

She took from her bag a folded envelope. Some leases of the late Miss Alice Harlow had fallen in; and by some oversight, as Mr Stebbings had found, they had not been included in the legacy. He tried to read the letter; tried hard to put out of his mind the all-important, the vital happening ... two grey eyes watching through a glass oval ... watching bundles of money in suitcases, in envelopes. ...

'Oh!' he said blankly. 'I see ... something about leases. I'll attend to that tomorrow.'

'Mr Harlow knows,' she said. 'We telephoned to him early this afternoon and he asked us to notify you and bring the particulars to his house tonight.'

At this he jerked up his head.

'You're going to Harlow – now?' he stammered.

It was rather remarkable that she had been looking forward to the visit all afternoon – very remarkable. The desire might seem incredible (and was) to the man who loved her. Yet, when Mr Stebbings had said in his incomplete way, 'I wonder if you would mind—' she had said promptly, 'No' – too promptly, she thought.

Reduced to its ignoble elements, the lure of Stratford Harlow was a perversity that could never be satisfied; the lure that brought timid people to the edge of a volcano to shudder and wonder at the molten pool that hissed and bubbled below. And something more than that, for he was less terrible than terribly human.

'Yes, I am going to Park Lane, now,' she said.

The mind of Mr Ellenbury was numb; he could not direct its working; it was without momentum, static.

'You are going to him now.'

Harlow had gone out of his way to meet this girl at Princetown; had made inquiries about her – where she lived, where she worked. He gave, as an excuse, his interest in her uncle. Ellenbury could, from common experience, find another. Those kinds of friendship develop very quickly. People who pass as strangers on the Monday may be planning a mutual future on the Saturday. A very pretty girl ...

the wheels of Mr Ellenbury's mind began to revolve, were soon whirling madly.

The first thing she would tell Harlow.

'Did you see Mr Ellenbury?'

'Yes; he had an enormous quantity of money in two suit-cases on his desk. ...'

He could imagine the swift conclusions that would follow.

'My wife is very ill' – the wheels creaked a little – 'very ill. She hasn't been out of bed for twenty years.' His weak mouth drooped pathetically. 'It is strange ... your coming like this. She asked about you this morning.'

'About me?' Aileen could hardly believe her ears. 'But I don't know her!'

'She knows you – knew you when you were a child – knew your mother or your father, I'm not sure which.' He was on safe ground here, though he was not sure of this. 'Curious. ... I intended calling at Stebbings's to ask you ... the car would bring you back.'

'To see Mrs Ellenbury – tonight?'

She was incredulous. Mr Ellenbury nodded his head.

'But – I've promised to go to Mr Harlow's house.'

'There will be time – it is an old man's request; unreasonable – I realise that.'

He looked very old and mean and unhappy.

'Is it far?'

He told her the exact position of this house – described the nearest route. What would happen after, he did not know. There would be time to consider that. Something dreadful. To keep her away from Harlow – her lover perhaps. That was the first consideration. His seats were booked, the cabin reserved; he left in the morning by the early train. Why not by Ostend? These by-thoughts insisted on confusing him.

'Could I telephone to Mr Stebbings?'

'I'll do that.' He was almost jovial. 'What you can do, young lady, is to help me pack these two cases. A lot of money, eh? All Harlow's, all Harlow's! A clever man!'

She nodded as she gathered up the bundles of bills.

'Yes – very clever.'

'A good fellow?'

She wasn't sure of this; he thought she was dissembling a new affection. Obviously she was fond of Harlow. Otherwise, since she was a known friend of Jim Carlton she must express her abhorrence. He had escaped a very real danger.

She had forgotten that he had promised to telephone until the car, waiting all this time in the soaking rain, was moving down Kingsway.

'I have a phone at my house,' he said.

It is true that he had a telephone – a private wire into Mr Harlow's library. But he was hardly likely to use it.

Crouched up in a corner of the car, the suitcases at his feet, knocking at his knees as the machine slowed or accelerated, he talked about his wife, but he thought of the girl by his side. And he reached this conclusion: she was the one person in the world who could betray him. The one person in the world who knew that he had two large suitcases filled with money. It was necessary that he should forget bank managers and Harlow and certain members of the Rata's staff, and so he forgot them. A bit of a girl to stand between him and a wonderful future. Picture galleries, sunlight on striped awnings, great masses of flowers blooming under blue skies, what time fog and rain clouds palled this filthy city and liquid mud splashed at the windows of the hired car.

They were nearing the house when he dropped the window and leaned out on the driver's side.

'The house is the fourth from the next side road. Stop before the gates; don't go into the drive and wait for a few minutes before you drive away.'

He pushed three notes into the man's hand: the gum-chewing driver examined them by the light on his instrument board and seemed satisfied.

'Do you mind if we stop at the gate? It is only a little

walk up the drive—my wife is so nervous; starts at every sound ...'

Aileen did not object. When they alighted in the muddy road, she offered to carry one of the cases and he consented. It was heavier than she expected.

'Harlow's, all Harlow's!' he muttered as he walked through the ugly gates and bent his head to the drive of rain. 'One of his "jokes".'

'What do you mean by "joke"?' she asked.

'Harlow's jokes ... difficult ... explain.' The wind tore words out of his speech.

She could see the house; square, lifeless.

'To the left – we go in at the back.'

They were following a cinder-path that ran snakily through the bare stems of rose bushes. Ahead of her she saw a squat building of some sort. It was the furnace house of the greenhouses, he told her.

'There are two steps down.'

Why on earth were they going into a hot-house at this time of night? He answered the question she had not put.

'Safe ... lock away ... cases,' he shouted.

The wind had freshened to a gale. A flicker of lightning startled her: lightning in December was a phenomenon outside her knowledge. Ellenbury put down the cases and pulled at a rusty padlock; a door groaned open.

'Here,' he said, and she went in after him.

He struck a match and lit an inch of candle in a grimy little storm-lantern and she could take stock of the place. It was a brick pit, windowless. The floor was littered with cinders and broken flower-pots. On a wooden bench was a heap of mould from which the green shoots of weed were sprouting. There was a rusting furnace door open and showing more ashes and cinders and garden rubbish.

'Just wait: I'll bring the bags.'

His heart was beating so violently that he could hardly breathe – fortunately for her peace of mind, she could not see his face.

He staggered out and slammed the door, threw the rusty lamp on to the staple and, groping at his feet, found the padlock and fixed it. Then he stumbled up the two steps and ran towards the house.

He had to sit on the steps for a long time before he was sufficiently calm to go in. Listening at the door before he opened it, he crept into the hall, closed the door without a sound and tiptoed to his study. He was wet through and shivering. The suitcases were shining like patent leather. He took off his drenched overcoat and rang the bell. The maid who presently appeared was surprised to see him.

'I thought, sir—' she began, but he cut her short.

'Go up to my room – don't make a noise – and bring me down a complete change. You may tell your mistress that I shall not be up for some time.'

Poking the meagre fire, he warmed his hands at the blaze. The girl came back with a bundle of clothes, announced her intention of making him a cup of tea and discreetly retired.

Mr Ellenbury started to change when a thought occurred to him. He might have to change again. His trousers were not very wet. And round about the pit was very muddy. He had thought of the pit in the car. Fate was working for him.

He put on his dressing-gown and took down from a shelf two volumes which he had often read. *The Chronicles of Crime* they were called – a record of drab evil told in the stilted style of their Early Victorian editor. They were each 'embellished with fifty-two illustrations by "Phiz".'

He opened a volume at random.

... when a female, young, beautiful and innocent, is the victim of oppression, there is no man with common feelings who would not risk his life to snatch her from despair and misery. ...

This little bit of moralising was the sentence he read. He turned the page, unconscious of its irony.

Maria Marten – shot in a barn. There was another woman killed with a sword. He turned the leaves impatiently; regretted at that moment so little acquaintance with the criminal bar. There was a large axe – where? Outside the kitchen door. He went down the kitchen stairs, passing the maid on her way up. Just outside the kitchen door, in the very place where he had seen it that morning, he found the axe. He brought it upstairs under his dressing-gown.

'You may go to bed,' he said to the maid. He drank his tea and then heard the ring of the telephone in the hall. He hesitated then hastened to answer it.

'Yes this is Ellenbury,' he strove to keep his voice calm, 'Miss Rivers? Yes she called at my office soon after six with a letter from Mr Stebbings – no I haven't seen her since ...'

He heaved on his wet overcoat and went out into the storm.

How very unpleasant! ... why couldn't they let him go away quietly ... an old man – white-haired, with only a few years to live? Tears rolled down his cheeks at the injustice of his treatment. It was Harlow! Damn Harlow! This poor girl, who had done nobody any harm – a beautiful creature who must die because of Harlow!

He dashed the weak tears from his eyes with the back of his hand, lifted off the padlock and threw open the door.

The candle had burnt down to its last flicker of life, but in that fraction of light, before the wick sank bluely into oblivion, he saw the white face of the girl as she stood, frozen with horror. Ellenbury swung his axe with a sob.

21

WHEN Mr Elk went into the office of his friend that afternoon, he found Jim engrossed in a large street plan that was spread out on the table. It had evidently been specially drawn or copied for his purpose, for there was a smudge of green ink where his sleeve had brushed.

'Buying house property?' asked Elk.

Jim rolled up the plan carefully and put it into his drawer.

'The real estate business,' Elk went on, 'is the easiest way of getting money I know. You can't be pinched for it, and there's no come-back. Friend of mine bought a cow field at Finchley and built a lot of ready-to-wear villas on it – he drives his own Jaguar nowadays. I know another man—'

'Would you like to assist me in a little burglary tonight?' interrupted Jim.

'Burglary is my long suit,' said Elk. 'I remember once—'

'There was a time,' mused Jim, 'when I could climb like a cat, though I've not seen a cat go up the side of a house, and I've never quite understood how "cat burglar" can be an apposite description.'

'Short for caterpillar,' suggested Elk. 'They can walk up glass owing to the suckers on their big feet. That's natural history, the same as flies. Where's the "bust"?'

'Park Lane, no less,' replied Jim. 'My scheme is to inspect one of the stately homes of England – the ancestral castle of Baron Harlow.'

'He ain't been knighted, has he?' asked Elk, who had the very haziest ideas about the peerage. 'Though I don't see why he shouldn't be; if—' he mentioned an illustrious political figure – 'was in office, Harlow would have been a duke by now, or an earl, or somethin'.'

Jim looked out of the window at the Thames Embankment, crowded at this rush hour with homeward-bound workers. It was raining heavily, and half a gale was blowing. Certainly the fog which had been predicted by the Weather Bureau showed no sign of appearance.

'The Weather people are letting me down,' he said; 'unless there's a fog we shall have to postpone operations till tomorrow night.'

Elk, who had certain views on the Weather Bureau, expressed them at length. But he had also something encouraging to say.

'Fog is no more use to a burglar than a bandaged eye.

Rain that keeps policemen in doorways and stops amacher snoopin' is weather from heaven for the burglar.'

Rain was falling in sheets on the Thames Embankment when the police car, which Jim Carlton drove, came through the arched gateway, and at the corner of Birdcage Walk he met a wind that almost overturned the car. He was blown across to Hyde Park Corner.

No. 704, Park Lane was one of the few houses in that thoroughfare which was not only detached from other houses but was surrounded by a wall. It could boast that beyond the library annexe was a small garden, in which a cherry tree flourished. A police sergeant detailed for the service appeared out of the murk and took charge of the car. In two minutes they were over the wall, dragging after them the hook ladder which had been borrowed during the afternoon from fire headquarters.

The domed skylight of the library was in darkness, and they gained its roof with little trouble. Here Jim left Elk as an advanced post. He had no illusions as to the difficulty of his task. All the upper windows were barred or secured by shutters; but he had managed to secure an aerial photograph which showed a little brick building on the roof, which was probably a stair cover and held a door that gave entrance to the floors below.

Jim drew himself up to the level of the first window, the bars of which made climbing a comparatively easy matter, and, detaching the hook of the ladder, he reached up and gripped the bars of the window above. Fortunately he was on the lee side of Greenhart House and the wind that shrieked about its corners did not greatly hamper him.

In ten minutes he was on the flat roof of the house, walking with difficulty in his felt-soled shoes towards the square brick shed. Now he caught the full force of the gale and was glad of the shelter which the parapet afforded.

As he had expected, in the brick superstructure there was a stout door, fastened by a patent lock. Probably it was bolted as well. He listened, but could hear nothing above the howl of the wind, and then continued his search of the roof, keeping the rays of his torch within a few inches of the ground. There was nothing to be discovered here, and he returned to the stairway. From his pocket he took a leather case of tools, fitted a small auger into a bit, and pushed it in the thickness of the door. He had not gone far before the point of the bit ground against something hard. The door was steel-lined. Replacing the tool, he pulled himself up to the roof of the shed, and he had to grip the edge to prevent being blown off.

The roof was of solid concrete, and it would need a sledge-hammer and unlimited time to break through.

Possibly there was an unguarded window, though he did not remember having seen any. He leaned across the parapet and looked down into the side street that connected Park Lane with the thoroughfare where he had left his car. As he did so, he saw a man walk briskly up to the door, open it and enter. The sound of the slamming door came up to him. It was obviously Harlow; no other man had that peculiar swing of shoulders in his walk. What had he been doing out on such a night? Then it occurred to Jim that he had come from the direction of his garage.

He heard a clock strike eleven. What should he do? It seemed that there was no other course but to return to the waiting Elk and confess his failure; and he had decided to take this action when he heard above the wind the snap of a lock being turned; and then the voice of Harlow. The man was coming up to the roof, and Jim crouched down in the shadow of the shed.

'. . . yes, it is raining, of course it is raining, my dear man. It is always raining in London. But I have been out in it and you haven't! Gosh, how it rained!'

Though the words themselves had a querulous tone, Mr Harlow's voice was good-humoured; it was as though he were speaking to a child.

'Have you got your scarf? That's right. And button your overcoat. You have no gloves, either. What a lad you are!'

⌐ 'I really don't want gloves,' said another voice. 'I am not a bit cold. And, Harlow, may I ask you again ...'

The voice became indistinct. They were walking away from the listener, and he guessed they were promenading by the side of the parapet. Unless Harlow carried a light he would not see the ladder. Jim went stealthily to the back of the shed and peered round the corner. Presently he discerned the figures of the two men: they were walking slowly towards him, their heads bent against the wind. Quickly he drew back again.

'... you can't have it. You are reading too much and I won't have your mind overtaxed by writing too much! Be reasonable, my dear Marling. ...'

Marling! Jim held his breath. They were so near to him now that by taking a step and stretching out his hand he could have touched the nearest man.

The lights in the street below gave him a sky-line against the parapet, and he saw that Harlow's companion was almost as tall as himself, save for a stoop. He caught a glimpse of a beard blown all ways by the gale. ... The voices came to him again as they returned; and then a sudden scraping sound and an exclamation from the financier.

'What the devil was that?'

From far below came a faint crash. Jim's heart sank. Harlow must have brushed against the hook ladder and knocked it from the parapet.

'You pushed something over,' said the stranger's voice.

'Felt like a hook,' said Harlow, and Jim could imagine him peering down over the parapet. 'What was it?' he said again.

This was Jim Carlton's opportunity. He could steal round the side of the building, slip through the door which he guessed was open, and make his escape. Noiselessly he crept along, and then saw a band of light coming from the open doorway. Against such a light he must be inevitably detected unless he chose a moment when their backs were turned. But they showed no inclination to move, and stood there for a time discussing the thing which Harlow had knocked from the stone coping.

'It's very curious' – the big man was talking – 'I don't remember there was anything when we came here this morning. Let us go down again.'

The opportunity was lost. Even as Jim stood there listening he heard the feet of the men descending the stairs, the crash of the door as it was closed. He was left on the roof without any means of making his way to solid earth.

To communicate with Elk was impossible without inviting discovery. He took a note-book from his pocket, wrote a hurried message and, tearing out the sheet, wrapped in it a copper coin. He dropped it as near as he could guess in the vicinity of the place where Elk would be, for he heard the tinkle of the copper as it struck the ground. A quarter of an hour he waited, but there was no sign from below. He tried the door again, without even hoping that it would afford him an exit. To his amazement, when he turned the handle the door opened. Had Harlow, in his hurried departure, forgotten to lock it? That was not like Harlow.

Jim pushed the door farther open and looked down. A dim light was burning in the room below, and he had a glimpse of a corner of the secretaire and a stretch of red carpet. Noiselessly he descended the stout stairs, which did not creak under his weight, and after a while, coming to the bottom, he peered round the lintel.

The room was apparently empty. A big desk stood near the curtained window; there was an empty lacquer bed in one corner, and, before him, a door which was ajar. The only light in the apartment came from the reading lamp on the desk – he crossed the room and, pressing the lamp switch, put the room in darkness.

A light on the landing outside was now visible round the edge of the door. He peeped out and could see no sign of life. Before him was a stairway which led down to the lower floors of the house. Something told him that his presence in the house was known. On the left of the landing was another door, and the first thing he noticed was that the key was in the lock. Whoever had opened and entered that room had gone in such haste that the key had not been removed. Jim saw his opportunity and in a flash, he leant over, gripped the key and snapped the lock tight. As he did so he heard a smothered exclamation from the room and grinned as he tiptoed down the stairs.

The lower landing was in darkness, and he could guide himself by his torch, testing every step he took, until he came into the dimly lighted vestibule, which, only a few days before, had been crowded with men and women, whose names were household words. He could hear nothing, and, walking swiftly to the door, grasped the handle. In another second he was flung back as though he had been struck by some huge invisible force.

He lay on the ground, breathless, paralysed with the shock. Then he heard the opening of a door upstairs, and somebody whispering. To touch that door handle, heavily charged with electric current, might mean death. The power which made the door a death trap for any burglar who succeeded in entering Harlow's house, must come off an existing connection, he thought. He saw the two white buttons jutting out of the wall, though only one light was visible in the hall. He pressed the top button back, but the hall light was not extinguished. This must be the connection. He tried the door handle again, touching it gingerly with his finger-tip. The current was off. In the briefest time he was in the street; and he advertised his escape by closing the door with a crash that shook the house.

Hurrying back to his car, he found Elk astride of the wall, in earnest parley with the police sergeant.

'I was just going round to the back to see what had happened to you,' said Elk, vaulting on to the sidewalk.

'Did you get my message?'

'What was it? I heard something fall, and thought you must have dropped the ladder. I couldn't locate it anyway.'

It was long past midnight when the driver stepped on his

brake before the entrance to Scotland Yard. And the first man Jim saw as he walked into the hall was Brown and his heart sank.

'Anything wrong?' he asked.

'Miss Rivers has not returned to the house,' said the detective. 'I've been on the 'phone to Stebbings. He tells me that she left at six o'clock to deliver two letters, one to Ellenbury and the other to Harlow. I got through to Ellenbury; he said his letter was handed to him by Miss Rivers soon after six and that he hadn't seen her since.'

Jim Carlton thought quickly.

'Just before eleven!' exclaimed Elk. 'Gosh! I'd forgotten that!'

'What?'

'That's the time he passed us and went into his garage – I could see the car from the top of the library – it wasn't his own and I didn't know it was Harlow until he turned into the gate at the end of the courtyard. And he was a long time in the garage too! I'll bet—'

It needed this clue, slight as it was, to spur Jim Carlton into instant action. At two o'clock in the morning, when Mr Harlow was finishing his last cigar, Jim Carlton and Elk arrived with the backing of a search warrant. ...

'How amusing!' said Mr Harlow sombrely, as he rose from the table and handed back the warrant to Jim.

'Do you mind letting me have a copy of that interesting document one of these days? I should like it for my autobiography!'

'You can save your breath, Harlow,' said Jim roughly. 'The present visit is nothing more than a little inconvenience for you. I'm not arresting you for the outrage on Sir Joseph Layton; I am not taking you for the murder of Mrs Gibbins!'

'Merciful as you are strong!' murmured Harlow. 'Murder is an unpleasant word.'

His face was rather pale and seemed to have developed new lines and furrows since Jim saw him last.

'What's this talk of murder?'

At the sound of the harsh voice the inspector spun round. Standing in the doorway was the hard-faced Mrs Edwins. It was the first time he had seen her, but he could recognise her instantly from Aileen's description. Stiffly erect, her arms folded before her, she stood waiting, her hard black eyes blazing with malignity. She was a more menacing figure then Harlow himself.

'What is this talk of murder? Who has been murdered, I should like to know?' she demanded.

But Harlow pointed past her.

' "Murder" was not your cue, Lucy Edwins,' he said pleasantly. 'Your sense of the dramatic will be your ruin!'

For a moment it seemed that the woman would disobey that imperious gesture. She blinked at him resentfully, almost with hate, and then turned, stiff as a ramrod, and disappeared.

'Now, Mr Carlton, let us be our calm selves. What do you expect to find in this house? I imagine it is something very important.'

'Imagine!' said Jim sternly. 'Harlow, I'm going to put my cards on the table and tell you just what I want to find. First and foremost, I want Aileen Rivers, who came here earlier in the evening with a letter from her employer. She has not been seen since.'

Mr Harlow did not smile.

'Really? Not been seen by you, I suppose you mean—'

'Wait, I haven't finished. A car was seen to drive away from Ellenbury's office in Theobald's Road at half-past five. Miss Rivers was in that car – where is she now?'

Harlow looked at him steadily.

'I will not say that I don't know – unnecessary lies are stupid.'

He opened a drawer of his desk with great deliberation, and, taking out a bunch of keys, dropped them on his blotting-pad.

'You may search every room in the house,' he said. 'And then tell me if you are as wise as I!'

The library itself needed no prolonged inspection. Jim went up the stairs, followed by Elk, and came at last to the top floor, to find Harlow waiting for him at the door of the little elevator.

'That is my housekeeper's room' – he pointed. 'You will recognise the door as the one which you locked a few hours ago.'

'And this?' asked Jim.

Harlow turned the handle and threw the other door wide open. The room was as Jim had seen it on the previous night, and was untenanted.

'We will start with the roof,' said Carlton, and went up the narrow flight of stairs, opened the door and stepped out onto the flat roof. This time he carried a powerful torch, but here also he drew blank. He made a circuit of the parapet and came back to where Harlow was waiting at the open door.

'Have you found a secret stairway?' Harlow was innocence itself. 'They are quite common in Park Lane, but still a novelty in Pimlico. You can touch a spring, something goes click, and there is a narrow winding stair leading to a still more secret room!'

Jim made no answer to this sarcasm, but went downstairs. From room to room he passed, but there was no sign of the girl or of the bearded man and at last he reached the ground floor.

'You have cellars? I should like to see them.'

Harlow opened a small door in the panelling of the vestibule. They were in a rather high, flagged passage, at the end of which was the kitchen and servants' hall. From an open archway in one of the walls a flight of stone stairs descended to the basement. This was made up of three cellars, two of which were used for the storage of wine.

'This is not the whole extent of the cellar space,' said Jim suspiciously, when he had finished his inspection.

'There are no other cellars,' replied Harlow, with a weary

sigh. 'My good man, how very suspicious you are! Would you like to see the garage?'

Jim followed him up the steps, through the hall.

He was being played with – Jim Carlton knew that, and yet for some reason was not rattled.

'Harlow, where is Miss Rivers? You suggested you knew.'

Harlow inclined his head graciously.

'If you will allow me to drive you a very little journey, I can promise that I will put an end to all your present doubts.'

They faced one another – Harlow towards the bright light that streamed from the garage.

'I'll call your bluff,' said Jim at last.

A slow smile dawned on Harlow's face.

'So many people have done that,' he said, 'and yet here I am, with a royal flush permanently in hand! And all who have called – where are their chips?'

He opened the car door and after a second's hesitation Jim entered, Mr Elk following. The big man shut the door.

'I have a high opinion of the police,' he said, 'and I realise that I am making you look rather foolish: I am sorry! This story of Harlow's penultimate joke shall go no farther than me.'

He moved away from the car and then very leisurely he walked to the wall, put up his hand, and the garage was in darkness.

Jim saw the manoeuvre and leapt to the door, but it was locked; and even as he struggled to lower the window, there was a whine of machinery and the car began to sink slowly through the floor. Down, down it went upon its platform and then, when the roof was a little below the level of the floor, the platform tilted forward, and the car slid gently onto an unseen track and thudded against rubber buffers and stopped.

Jim had got the window down and was half through when the hydraulic pillars beneath the platform shot up and closed the aperture with a gentle thud. In another second Elk was free. Wrenching open the driver's door, Jim switched on the powerful head lamps and illuminated the chamber to which the car had sunk.

There were two more machines there; one in particular attracted his attention – an old hire car grey with mud which was still wet. Evidently the place was a very ordinary type of underground garage, though he had never seen such expensive equipment as a hydraulic lift in a private establishment. The walls were of dressed stone; at one end was a low iron door, not locked, so far as he could see, but fastened with two steel bolts. It was probably a petrol store, he thought, and the position under the courtyard before the garage confirmed this guess.

He looked at Elk.

'How foolish do *you* feel?' he asked bitterly.

Elk shook his head.

'Nothin' makes me feel foolish,' he said cheerfully, 'but I certainly didn't expect to see the end so soon.'

'End?'

Elk nodded.

'Not mine – not yours: Harlow's. He's through – what's penultimate mean, anyway?'

And when it was explained, Elk's face brightened.

'He's got one big line to finish on? I'll bet it is the biggest joke that's ever made the police stop laffin. And I'll tell you—'

He stopped; both heads went round towards the little iron door. Somebody was knocking feebly and Jim's heart almost stopped beating.

'Somebody behind that door,' said Elk. 'I never thought old man Harlow ran a dungeon.'

Jim ran to the place, slipped back the bolts and flung the iron door open – there staggered into the light the wild and dishevelled figure of an elderly man. For a moment Jim did not recognise him. He was coatless, his crumpled collar was unfastened, but it was the look in his face that transfixed the astonished men.

'Ellenbury!' breathed Jim.

The lawyer it was, but the change in him since Jim had seen him last was startling. The wide opened eyes glared from one to the other and then he raised his trembling hand to his mouth.

'Where is she?' he whispered fiercely. 'What did he do with her?'

Jim's heart turned to lead.

'Who – Miss Rivers?'

Ellenbury peered at him as though he remembered his voice but could not identify him.

'Stebbings's girl!' he croaked. 'He took the axe – Harlow!' The old man swung an imaginary axe. 'Ugh! ... killed her!'

Jim Carlton's hand was thrust to the wall for support. His face was colourless – he could not speak and it was Elk who took up the questioning of this apparition.

'Killed her?'

Ellenbury nodded.

'Where—?'

'On the edge of the kitchen garden ... there's a pit. You could put somebody there and nobody would guess. He knew all about the pit. I didn't know he was the chauffeur – he had a little black moustache and he'd been driving me all day.'

Elk laid his hand gently on the little man's shoulder and he shrank back with a sound of weeping.

'Listen, Mr Ellenbury, you must tell us all you know and try to be calm. Nobody will hurt you. Did he kill Miss Rivers?'

The man nodded violently.

'With an axe – my axe ... I saw her lying there on the furnace-room floor. She was very beautiful and white and I saw that he had killed her and went back to the house for I did not wish – I did not wish ...' he shuddered, his face in his hands, 'to see her in that pit, with the water ... green water ... ugh ... ugh!'

He was fighting back the vision, his long fingers working like a piano player's.

'Yes ... you saw her again?' asked Jim huskily.

He had.

'Where?'

'In the back of the car – where the suitcases were – all huddled up on the floor with a blanket thrown over her. I sat beside the devil and he talked! So softly! God! You'd have thought he had never murdered anybody! He said he was going to take me for a holiday – where I'd get well. But I knew he was lying – I knew the devil was lying and that he was forging new links in my chain. He put me in there!'

He almost screamed the words as his wavering finger pointed to the open door of his prison.

'Ellenbury, for God's sake try to think – is Aileen Rivers alive?'

The old man shook his head.

'Dead!' he nodded with every repetition of the word, 'dead, dead, dead! My axe ... it was outside the kitchen door ... I saw her lying there and there was blood ...'

'Listen, Carlton,' it was Elk's harsh voice. 'I'm not believing this! This bird's mad—'

'Mad! Am I mad!' Ellenbury struck his thin chest. 'She's upstairs – I saw him carry her up – and the woman with the yellow face, and the man with a beard ... they made me come with them ... left me here in the dark for a long time and then made me come with them – look!'

He dragged Elk into the little prison house. There was a bed and a wardrobe; carpet covered the floor. It was a self-contained little suite, in the depth of the cellar.

Fumbling on the wall he found a light switch and the room was flooded with a rose-coloured glow that came from concealed lights in the angle of a stone cornice.

'Look – look!'

The lawyer dragged open the door of the wardrobe. At the bottom was a heap of clothes – men's clothes. A crumpled dress shirt, a velvet dress-jacket—

'Sir Joseph's clothes!' gasped Elk.

22

'THEY KEPT him here,' whispered Ellenbury. He seemed afraid of the sound of his own voice.

Jim saw another steel door at the farther end of the room; it had no bolt – only a tiny keyhole. And then his attention was diverted.

'Look!' called Ellenbury.

Exercising all his strength, the little man pulled at the wardrobe and it swung out like a gate on a hinge. Behind was an oblong door.

'There ... I came that way. The elevator ...'

As Elk listened, he heard the distant whine of the elevator in motion.

'To what room did he take her?' asked Jim huskily. 'We searched everywhere.'

'Mrs Edwins'. There is a cupboard, but the back is a false one. There is a small room behind ... why didn't they put her in the pit and hide her? It would have been better ...'

'We've got to get out of here, and quick,' said Elk, and looked round for the means of escape. 'Penultimate joke hasn't raised a laugh yet – looks like the penultimate joke's goin' to put my relations in mournin'!'

He tried to climb one of the greasy hydraulic cylinders, but although, with the assistance of Jim, he managed to touch the platform, he could derive little comfort from his achievement. The platform was of steel and concrete. Neither knew anything of the mechanism of an hydraulic lift, and indeed the controls were out of reach under a locked steel grating.

The door behind the wardrobe was the only possible means of egress. Elk searched the car, and the tool chest beneath.

'We're safe for a bit – he'd be scared of using any kind of gas for fear there was a blow-up and he hasn't the means of manufacturing something quick and sudden. Carlton, did you notice anything in the house!'

'I noticed many things. To which do you refer?

'Notice that we never saw Mrs Edwins or Edwards, or whatever her name was, after the old man said "get"!'

That fact had not occurred to Jim; though they had searched the house from roof to basement, he had not seen the hard-faced woman again.

'Where she is,' said Elk, 'the other feller can be – what's 'is name – Marling? And I know pretty well where that was – in the little elevator!'

It was true! Jim had seen the elevator when Harlow waited upon the top floor, but after that it had disappeared. It was the easiest thing in the world to slip from floor to floor, missing the search party.

The door was immovable; he could secure no leverage, and even if he had, it was unlikely that it would yield.

They must attack the concrete-covered brickwork. This was the only section of the wall that was not built of stone. Fortunately for them, there were tool chests in all the cars, and moreover in one of the machines was a big car jack, the steel lever of which they disconnected and used as a crowbar.

The work was an anodyne to Jim Carlton's jangled nerves, set further on edge every time he saw the white face of Ellenbury.

The lawyer crouched by the bed watching them and muttering all the time under his breath. Once, in a pause, Jim heard him say:

'You can't measure principles with a yard stick; such a beautiful girl! And very young!' And then he started weeping softly.

'Don't notice him,' snarled Elk; 'get on with the work!'

To move only an inch of concrete was an arduous and difficult business, and not without its danger if the sound were heard by the master of the house. But after an hour's work they cleared a square foot of the hard plaster and revealed the brick lining beneath. Using screwdrivers for chisels, they managed to dislodge the first brick in the course and enlarge the hole. The second brick course was easier; but now the necessity for caution was brought home to them dramatically.

Jim was fitting the jagged edge of his driver into a small hole in the mortar, when a muffled voice almost at his elbow said:

'Leave them alone: they can wait until tomorrow.'

It was Harlow, and Jim almost jumped.

But the phenomenon had a simple explanation. His voice had been carried down the shaft of the lift. They heard a gate slam, again came the whine of the motor and the lift stopped just above them, the gate was fastened again, and by a trick of acoustics Jim could hear the man's foot tapping on the tiled floor of the vestibule.

They had till the morning; that was a comfort. Working and listening at intervals, they dislodged the inner brick, drew it out, a second followed, and in half an hour there was a jagged hole through which a lean man might wriggle. Jim was that lean man. He found himself in the greasy pit of the elevator shaft, stumbling over beams and pulleys in a darkness which was unrelieved by a single ray from above. He reached back into the room for his torch and made an inspection. The bottom of the lift was at least twelve feet above where he stood and hanging from it were two thick electric cables. Reaching up, he could just touch the lowest of the loops. He told Elk the position, and all the car cushions that could be gathered were thrust through the hole and piled by Jim, one on top of the other.

Balancing himself on these, he took a steady grip of the cable and rested his weight. The wires held. Pulling himself up, hand over hand, he managed to reach a thick steel bar which connected with the safety brake, and began to push the elevator floor, hoping to find a trap door. But evidently this little lift was too small for a mechanic's trap, the floor did not yield under his pressure, and he was debating whether he should drop on to the cushions when he heard a quick step in the vestibule, a heavy foot stepped into the lift and the door slammed to. In another second he was mounting rapidly. On the top floor the lift stopped with a jerk which almost loosened his hold, though he had braced his feet upon the dangling cables below.

The upper floors were not as deep as the two lower. As he hung, his knee was on a level with the top of the elevator entrance to the second floor. There was a footledge there, and if he could reach it, it would be a simple matter to climb over the tiny grille. It was worth trying. Gently he slid down the cable until, swinging his feet, he could just touch the six inches of floor space between the pit and the grille. Then, concentrating all his strength, he leapt forward, snatching at the breast-high gate – his feet slipping from under him. He recovered in a second, and was over the top.

He crept noiselessly up the stairs and was almost detected by the tall woman who was standing on the landing, her ear to the closed door of the room in which, he suspected, Aileen was a prisoner. From where he stood, concealed by a turn of the stairs, he could hear Harlow's voice raised in complaint.

'It was so vulgarly theatrical! I'm not annoyed, I'm hurt! To write messages on a card was stupid ... and with a pin. If I had known ...'

There was an agitated, murmured reply, and then unexpectedly Harlow laughed.

'Well, well, you're a foolish fellow; that is all I have to say to you. And you must never do such a thing again. Luckily the police couldn't read your writing.'

Jim had almost forgotten the existence of the bearded man. He heard the door open and went quickly down the stairs until he was in the vestibule. The hands of the little silver clock over the marble mantelpiece pointed to five.

The lift was coming down again, and crouching back into

a recess, Jim saw the big man pass into the library. The door shut behind him.

In a second the detective was in the elevator and had pressed the top button.

If Aileen were there, he would find her; he dare not allow himself even to debate the sanity of the little man he had left in the garage.

Was she here? ... dead?

He closed his eyes to shut out the dreadful picture that the lawyer had drawn ... the axe ... the pit ...

Just as the elevator reached the top floor something happened.

For a few seconds Carlton did not grasp the explanation. The two lights in the roof of the lift went out, and down below something flashed bluely – Jim saw the lightning flicker of it.

He pushed at the grille which, on the top floor alone, reached from ceiling to floor. It did not budge. He kicked at the gates, but they were of hammered steel.

Trapped for a second time in three hours. Jim swore softly through his teeth. He heard the street door close below and silence.

'Elk!'

From a distance came Elk's hollow answer.

'He has cut out a fuse – can you climb to the hall?'

'I'll try.'

Facing where he stood, caged and impotent, was the door of Mrs Edwins' room and as he looked he saw the handle turning slowly ... slowly.

Mrs Edwins? She had been left behind then. ...

The door opened a little ... a little more, and then Aileen Rivers walked out.

'Aileen!' he cried hoarsely.

She looked at him, gripping the gate, his haggard face against the bars.

'The philandering constable,' she said, bravely flippant; and then, 'please – take me home!'

'Who brought you here?' he asked, hardly believing the evidence of his senses.

'I came of my own free will – oh, Jim he's such a darling!'

'Oh, God!' groaned the man in the cage, 'and I never noticed it!'

23

NEARLY TWELVE hours before that poignant moment a gum-chewing chauffeur had found himself in an awkward position.

'A lunatic and a fainting female!' mused the chauffeur. 'This is most embarrassing!'

Stooping, he lifted the girl and laid her limply over his shoulder. With his disengaged hand he dragged the dazed old lawyer to his feet.

'You hit me!' whimpered Ellenbury.

'You are alive,' said the chauffeur loftily, 'which is proof that I did not hit you.'

'You choked me!'

The chauffeur uttered a tut of impatience.

'Go ahead, Bluebeard!' he said.

Apparently one hundred and forty pounds of femininity was not too great a tax on the chauffeur's strength, for as he walked behind the weeping little man, one hand on the scruff of his collar, he was whistling softly to himself.

Up the stone steps he walked and into the hall. The ancient maid came peeping round the corner, and almost fell down the kitchen stairs in her excitement, for something was happening at Royalton House – where nothing had happened before.

The chauffeur lowered the girl into a little armchair. Her eyes were open; she was feeling deathly ill.

'There is nothing in the world like a cup of tea,' suggested the chauffeur, and called in the maid, so imperiously that she never even glanced at her master. He seemed dwindled in stature. In his hand he still held the wet haft of the axe. He was rather a pathetic little man.

'I think you had better put that axe away,' said the chauffeur gently.

Aileen only then became aware of his presence. He had a funny moustache, walrus-like and black, and as he spoke it waggled up and down. She wanted to laugh, but she knew that laughter was half-way to hysteria. Her eyes wandered to the axe; a cruel-looking axe – the handle was all wet and slippery. With a shiver she returned her attention to the chauffeur; he was holding forth in an oracular manner that reminded her of somebody. She discovered that he was watching her too, and this made her uneasy.

'You've got to help me, young lady,' said the man gravely.

She nodded. She was quite willing to help him, realising that she would not be alive at that moment but for him.

The chauffeur rolled his eyes round to Ellenbury.

'O, what a tangled web we weave,
When first we practise to deceive!'

he said reproachfully; and stripped his black moustache with a grimace of pain.

'Thank God that's gone!' he said, and pulled up a chair to the fire. 'I was once very useful to Nova – Nova has this day paid his debt and lost a client. Why don't you take off your overcoat? It's steaming.'

He glanced at the axe, its wet haft leaning against the fireplace and then, reaching out his hand, took it on to his knees and felt its edge.

'Not very sharp, but horribly efficient,' he said, and laid his hand on the shoulder of the shrinking man. 'Ellenbury, my man, you've been dreaming!'

Ellenbury said nothing.

'Nasty dreams, eh? My fault. I had you tensed up – I should have let you down months ago.'

Now Ellenbury spoke in a whisper.

'You're Harlow?'

'I'm Harlow, yes.' He scarcely gave any attention to the two suitcases; one glance, and he did not look at them again. 'Harlow the Splendid. The Robber Baron of Park Lane. There's a good title for you if you ever write that biography of mine!'

Mr Harlow glanced round at the girl and smiled; it was a very friendly smile.

Ellenbury offered no resistance when the big man relieved him of his wet coat and held up the dressing-gown invitingly.

'Take off your shoes.'

The old man obeyed; he always obeyed Harlow.

'When are you leaving?'

'Tomorrow,' the admission was wrung from him. He had no resistance.

'One suitcase full of money is enough for any man,' said Harlow. 'I'll take a chance – you shall have first pick.'

'It's yours!' Ellenbury almost shouted the words.

'No – anybody's. Money belongs to the man who has it. That is my pernicious doctrine – you will go to Switzerland, get as high up the mountains as you can. St Moritz is a good place. Very likely you're mad. I think you are. But madness cannot be cured by daily association with other madmen. It would be stupid to hide you up in an asylum – stupid and wicked. And if you will not think of killing people any more, Ellenbury. You – are – not – to – think – about – killing!'

'No!'

The old man was weeping foolishly.

'Our friend Ingle leaves for the Continent tomorrow – join him. If he starts talking politics, pull the alarm cord and have him arrested. I don't know where he is going – anywhere but Russia, I guess. ...'

All the time he was talking, Aileen sensed his anxiety. Just then the maid brought in the tea and the big fellow relaxed.

'Drink that hot,' he ordered, and when the servant had gone he moved nearer to the girl and lowered his voice.

'He doesn't respond. You noticed that? No reflexes, I'm certain. I dare not try; he'd think I was assaulting him. It was my own fault. I kept him too tense – too keyed up. If I had let him down ... umph!'

He shook his head; the thick lips pursed and drooped. Presently he spoke again.

'I'll have to bring you both away – you can be very helpful. If you insist upon going to Carlton and telling him about ... this' – he nodded to the unconscious man by the fire – 'I shan't stop you. This is the finish, anyway.'

'Of what?' she asked.

'Harlow the Joker,' he said. 'Don't you see that? Here's a man who tried to murder you – a madman. Why? Because he thought you knew he was bolting. Here's Harlow the magnificent masquerading like a fiction detective with a comic moustache! Why? Imagine the police asking all these questions. And Ellenbury of course would tell them quite a lot of things – some silly, some sane. The police are rather clever – not very, but rather. They'd smell – all sorts of jokes. I want a day if I can get it. Would you come to Park Lane for a day?'

'Willingly!' she said; and he went red.

'That is a million-pound compliment,' he said. 'You'll have to sit on the floor with a rug over you; you musn't be seen. As it is, if you are missed, your impetuous lover – did you speak?'

'I didn't,' she said emphatically.

'If he learns that you have disappeared, my twenty-four hours will be shortened.'

She glanced at Ellenbury.

'What shall you do with ... him?' she asked.

'He sits by my side; I dare not leave him here.'

He lifted up one of the suitcases and weighed it in his hand.

'Would you like half a million?' he asked pleasantly.

Aileen shook her head.

'I don't think there is much happiness in that money,' she said.

He laughed.

'Forgive me! I've got a little joke at the back of my mind – maybe I'll tell you all about it!'

24

SHE TOLD Jim all about this as he drove her back to her rooms after she had brought a policeman to release him.

'He *is* rather a darling,' she repeated, and when he frowned she pressed his arm and laughed. 'Somehow I don't think you will arrest him,' she said. 'But if you do, hold him very tight!'

And she thought of Mr Harlow's joke.

When, an hour later, a strong force of plain-clothes policemen descended upon 704 Park Lane, they found only Mrs Edwins, erect and intractable as ever, her hands folded over her waist.

'Mr Harlow left for the country this morning,' she said, and when they searched the house they discovered neither the Splendid Harlow nor the golden-bearded man called Marling.

'Arrest me!' she sneered. 'It takes a clever policeman to arrest an old woman. But you'll not take Lemuel.'

'Lemuel?'

She realised her mistake.

'I called him Lemuel when he was a child, and I call him Lemuel now,' she said defiantly. 'He'll ruin every one of you – mark my words!'

She was still muttering threats when two detectives found her coat and hat and led her, protesting, to the police station.

Mr Harlow's landed possessions were not limited to his *pied-à-terre* in Park Lane. He had a large estate in Hampshire, which he seldom visited, though he retained a considerable staff for its upkeep. It was known that he owned a luxurious flat in Brighton; and it was generally believed that somewhere in London he kept another extensive suite of apartments.

Stratford Harlow was a far-thinker. He saw not only tomorrow but the day after. For over twenty years he had lived in the knowledge that he was a reprehensible jester, and that there was always a possibility, if not a probability, that his supreme 'joke' would be detected.

He was at the mercy of many men, for only the mean thief may work single-handed. He had perforce to employ people who must be taken – a little – into his confidence. But only one person knew the big truth.

His chauffeur, who knew so much, never dreamt the whole; to Ellenbury he had been a crooked market-rigger; to Ingle he had been an admirable enemy of society. To himself, what was he? That 'joke' idea persisted; almost the description fitted his every action. When he had locked the grille on Jim he knew that the 'joke' was on him. The machinery of the law had begun to move, and there was nothing to be gained by dodging from one hiding place to another. It was a case of flight or nothing.

He went to the foot of the stairs and whistled; and soon Mrs Edwins came into view with the tall, bearded man.

'Marling, I am going to take you for a little drive,' said Stratford Harlow pleasantly. 'You are at once a problem and a straw. You have almost broken my neck and I am grasping at you.' He laughed gently. 'That's a mixed illustration, isn't it?'

'Where are you going?' asked Mrs Edwins.

He fixed her with his cold eyes.

'You are very inquisitive and very stupid,' he said. 'What is worse, you lack self-control, and that has nearly been my undoing. Not that I blame you.' A gesture of his white hand absolved her from responsibility. 'Telephone to Reiss to bring the car. Possibly he will telephone in reply that he is unable to bring the car. You may even hear the strange and authoritative voice of a policeman.'

Her jaw dropped.

'You don't mean?' she asked quickly.

'Please telephone.'

He was very patient and cheerful. He did not look at her; his eyes, lit with a glint of humour, focused upon the uncomfortable man who faced him.

'I hope I've done nothing—' began Marling.

'Nothing at all – nothing!' said Mr Harlow with the greatest heartiness. 'I have told you before, and I tell you again, you have nothing to fear from me. You are a victim of circumstances, incapable of a wrong action. I would sooner die than that you suffered so much as a hurt! Injustice pains me. That variety of justice which is usually called "poetical" fills me with a deep and abiding peace of soul. Well?' He snapped the question at the woman in the doorway.

'What am I to do with that girl?' she asked.

'Leave her alone,' said the big man testily, 'and at the earliest opportunity restore her to her friends. Help Mr Marling on with his coat; it is a cold night. And a scarf for his throat ... Good!'

He peered through the ground-glass window.

'Reiss has brought the car. Trustworthy fellow,' he said, and beckoned Marling to him. Together they left the house and were driven rapidly away. For nearly a quarter of an hour Mrs Edwins stood in the deserted vestibule, very upright, very forbidding, her gnarled hands folded, staring at the door through which they had passed.

The car drove through Mayfair, turned into a side street and stopped. It was a corner block, the lower floor occupied by a bank. There was a side door, which Mr Harlow opened and stood courteously aside to allow his companion to pass. They went up a long flight of stairs to another door, which Harlow unlocked.

'Here we are, my dear fellow,' he said, closing the door

gently. 'This is what is called a labour-saving flat; one of those modern creations designed by expensive architects for the service of wealthy tenants who are so confoundedly mean that they weigh out their servants' food! Here we shall live in comparative quiet for a week or two.'

'What has happened?' asked Marling.

The big man shrugged his shoulders.

'I do not know – I rather imagine that I recognise the inevitable, but I am not quite sure. Your room is here, at the back of the house. Do you mind?'

Marling saw that it was a more luxurious apartment than that which he had left. Books there were in plenty. The only drawback was that the windows were covered with a thin coating of white paint which made them opaque.

'I prepared this place for you two, nay, three years ago,' said Harlow. 'For a week or two, until we can make arrangements, I am afraid we shall have to do our own housework.'

He patted the other on the shoulder.

'You're a good fellow,' he said. 'There are times when I would like to change places with you. *Vivit post funera virtus*! I, alas! have no virtues, but a consuming desire to make wheels turn.'

He pursed his thick lips and then said, apropos of nothing:

'She is really a very nice girl indeed! ... And she has a sense of humour. How rare a quality in a woman!'

'Of whom are you talking?' asked the bearded man, a little bewildered.

'The might-have-been,' was the flippant reply. 'Even the wicked cannot be denied their dreams. Would you call me a sentimentalist, Marling?'

Marling shook his head, and Mr Harlow laughed not unkindly.

'You're the most appallingly honest man I've ever met,' he said, in admiration; 'and I think you're the only human being in the world for whom I have a genuine affection.'

His companion stared at him with wide-open eyes. And Mr Harlow met the gaze without faltering. He was speaking the truth. His one nightmare in the past twenty years was that this simple soul should fall ill; for if that catastrophe had occurred, Stratford Harlow would have risked ruin and suffering to win him back to health. Marling was the only joke in life that he took seriously.

Every morning for three years, two newspapers had been thrust under the door of Harlow's flat and had been disposed of by the hired servant who came to keep the place in order. Every morning a large bottle of milk had been deposited on the mat and had been similarly cleared away by the servant, who would come no more, for she had received a letter dispensing with her services on the morning Harlow and his companion arrived. The letter was not signed 'Stratford Harlow,' but bore the name by which she knew her employer.

The first day was a dull one. Harlow had nothing to do and inactivity exasperated him. He was down early the next morning to take in milk and newspapers; and for a long time sat at his ease, a thin cigar between his teeth, a cup of cooling coffee by his side, reading of his disappearance. The ports were watched; detectives were on duty at the termini of all airways. The flying squad was scouring London. The phrase seemed familiar. The flying squad from police headquarters spend their lives scouring London, and London seems none the cleaner for it.

There was his portrait across three columns, headed 'The Splendid Harlow,' and only hinting at the charge which would be laid against him. He learnt, without regret or sorrow, of the arrest of Mrs Edwins – he had a lifelong grudge against Mrs Edwins, who had a lifelong grudge against him. She was wholly incapable of understanding his attitude to life. She had wondered why he did not live abroad in the most luxurious and exotic atmosphere. She would have excused a seraglio; she could not forgive his industry and continence.

She had made no statement, the newspapers said, and

he suspected her of making many of a vituperative character. There was a hint of Marling in the paragraph:

The police are particularly desirous of getting into touch with the man who left the Park Lane house at the same time as Harlow. He is described as tall, rather pale, with a long yellow beard. None of the servants of the house has ever seen him. It may be explained that Mr Harlow's domestic arrangements were of an unusual character. All the servants slept out in a house which Harlow had hired . . .

Mr Harlow turned over the page to see the sporting cartoon. The humour of Tom Webster never failed to amuse him. Then he turned back to the Stock Exchange news. Markets were recovering rapidly. He made a calculation on the margin of the paper and purred at his profits.

He could feel a glow of satisfaction though he was a fugitive from justice; though all sorts of horrid possibilities were looming before him; though it seemed nothing could prevent his going the dreary way – Brixton Prison, Pentonville, Wormwood Scrubbs, Dartmoor . . . if not worse. If not worse.

He took out his cigar and looked at it complacently. Mrs Gibbins had died a natural death, though that would take some proving. It was a most amazingly simple accident. Her muddy shoes had slipped on the polished floor of his library; and when he had picked her up she was dead. That was the truth and nothing but the truth. And Miss Mercy Harlow had died naturally; and the little green bottle that Marling had seen had contained nothing more noxious than the restorative with which the doctor had entrusted him against the heart attack from which she succumbed.

He rose and stretched himself, drank the cold coffee with a wry face, and shuffled along leisurely in his slippered feet to call Saul Marling. He knocked at the door, but there was no answer. Turning the handle, he went in.

The room was empty. So, too, was the bathroom.

Mr Harlow walked along the passage to the door leading down to the street. It was open. So also was the street door.

He stood for a while at the head of the stairs, his hands in his pockets, the dead cigar between his teeth. Then he descended, closed the door and, walking back to the sitting-room, threw the cigar into the fire-place, lit another and sat down to consider matters; his forehead wrinkled painfully. Presently he gave utterance to the thought which filled his mind.

'I do hope that poor fellow is careful how he crosses the road – he isn't used to traffic!'

But there were policemen who would help a timid, bearded man across the busy streets, and it was rather early for heavy traffic.

That thought comforted him. He took up the newspaper and in a second was absorbed in the Welbury divorce case which occupied the greater part of the page.

25

AILEEN RIVERS might well have excused herself from attending her office, but she hated the fuss which her absence would occasion; and she felt remarkably well when she woke at noon.

Mr Stebbings greeted her as though she had not been absent until lunch-time, to his great inconvenience; and one might not imagine, from his matter-of-fact attitude, that he had been badgered by telephone messages and police visitations during the twelve hours which preceded her arrival.

He made no reference to her adventure until late in the afternoon, when she brought in some letters for him to sign. He put his careful signature to each sheet and then looked up.

'James Carlton comes of a very good family. I knew his father rather well.'

She went suddenly red at this and was for the moment so thrown off her balance that she could not ask him what James Carlton's parentage had to do with a prosaic and involved letter on the subject of leases.

'He was most anxious about you, naturally,' Mr Stebbings

rambled on aimlessly. 'I was in bed when he called me up – I have never heard a man who sounded so worried. It is curious that one does not associate the police force with those human emotions which are common in us all, and I confess it was a great surprise – in a sense a gratifying surprise! I have seen him once; quite a goodlooking young man; and although the emoluments of his office are not great, he appeals to me as one who has the capacity of making any woman happy.' He paused. 'If women can be made happy,' he added, the misogynist in him coming to the surface.

'I really don't know what you mean, Mr Stebbings,' she said, very hot, a little incoherent, but not altogether distressed.

'Will you take this letter?' said Mr Stebbings, dismissing distracted detectives and hot-faced girls from his mind; and immediately she was plunged into the technology of an obscure trusteeship which the firm of Stebbings was engaged in contesting.

As Aileen grew calmer, the shock of the discovery grew in poignancy. A girl who finds herself to be in love experiences a queer sense of desolation and loneliness. It is an emotion which seems unshareable; and the more she thought of Jim Carlton, the more she was satisfied that the affection was one-sided; that she was wasting her time and thought on a man who did not care for her any more than he cared for every other girl he met; and that love was a disease which was best cured by fasting and self-repression.

She was in this frame of mind when there came a gentle tap at her door. She called 'Come in!' – the handle turned and a man walked nervously into the room. A tall man, hatless, collarless, and inadequately clad. An overcoat many times too broad for him was buttoned up to the neck, and although he wore shoes he was sockless and his legs were covered by a pair of dark-blue pyjamas. He stroked his long beard nervously and looked at the girl in doubt.

'Excuse me, madam,' he said, 'is this the office of Stebbings, Field and Farrow?'

She had risen in amazement.

183

'Yes. Do you wish to see Mr Stebbings?'

He nodded, looked nervously round at the door and closed it behind him.

'If you please,' he said.

'What name?' she asked.

He drew a long breath.

'Will you tell him that Mr Stratford Harlow wishes to see him?'

Her mouth opened in amazement.

'Stratford Harlow? Is he here?'

He nodded.

'I am Stratford Harlow,' he said simply.

The gentleman who for twenty-three years had borne the name of Stratford Harlow was drinking a cup of China tea when the bell rang. He finished the tea, and wiped his mouth with a silk handkerchief. Again the bell shrilled. Mr Harlow rose with a smile, dusted the crumbs from his coat and, pausing in the passage to take down an overcoat and a hat from their pegs, walked down the stairs and threw open the door.

Jim Carlton was standing on the sidewalk, and with him three gentlemen who were unmistakably detectives.

'I want you, Harlow,' he said.

'I thought you might,' said Mr Harlow pleasantly. 'Is that your car?' He patted his pockets. 'I think I have everything necessary to a prisoner of state. You may handcuff me if you wish, though I would prefer that you did not. I do not carry arms. I regard any man who resists arrest by the use of weapons as a cowardly barbarian! For the police have their duties – very painful duties sometimes, pleasant duties at others – I am not quite sure in which category yours will fall.'

Elk opened the car door and Mr Harlow stepped in, settled himself comfortably in the corner and asked:

'May I smoke?'

He produced a cigar from his coat pocket and Elk held the light as the car moved towards Evory Street.

'There is one thing I would like to ask you, Carlton,' he

said, half-turning his head towards his captor, who sat by his side. 'I read in the newspapers that the ports and airports were being watched and all sorts of extraordinary precautions were being taken against my leaving the country. I presume that the news of my arrest will be made known immediately to these watchful gentlemen? I should hate to feel that they were tramping up and down in the cold, looking for a man who was already in custody. That would spoil my night's sleep.'

Jim humoured his mood.

'They will be notified,' he said.

'You found Marling, of course? He has suffered no injury? I am very relieved. It is difficult to conceive the confusion which must arise in the mind of a man who has been out of the world for some twenty years and returns to find the streets so crowded with death-dealing automobiles, driven usually at a pace beyond the legal limit.'

'Yes, Mr Harlow is in good hands.'

'Call him Marling,' said the other. 'And Marling he must remain until my duplicity is proved beyond any question. I will make the matter easy for you by admitting that he is Stratford Selwyn Mortimer Harlow.'

He went off at a tangent, a trick of his.

'I should have gone away a long time ago and defied you to bring home to me any offence against the law. But I am intensely curious – if my dearest wish were realised, I would be suspended in a condition of disembodied consciousness to watch the progress of the world through the next two hundred thousand years! I would like to see what new nations arise, what new powers overspread the earth, what new continents will be pushed up from the sea and old continents submerged! Two hundred thousand years. There will be a new Rome, a new barbarian Britain, a new continent of America populated by indescribable beings! New Ptolemys and Pharaohs getting themselves embalmed; and never dreaming that their magnificent tombs shall be buried under sand and forgotten until they are dug out to be gaped at by tourists, who will pay two piastres a peep!'

He sighed, flicked the ash of his cigar onto the floor of the car.

'Well, here I am at the end. I've seen it out. I know now into which compartment the little whirling ball of fate has fallen. It is extremely interesting.'

They hurried him into the charge-room and put him in the steel pen; and he beamed round the room.

In an undertone to Jim he said:

'Can anything be done to prevent the newspapers with one accord describing what they will call the "irony" of my appearance in a police station which I presented to the nation? Almost I am tempted to present a million pounds to the journal which refrains from this obvious comment!'

He listened in silence to the charge which Elk read, interrupting only once.

'Suspected of causing the death of Mrs Gibbins? How perfectly absurd! However, that is a matter for the lawyers to thrash out.'

With the jailer's hand on his arm he disappeared to the cells.

'And that's that!' said Jim, with a heartfelt sigh of relief.

'Where's the real fellow?' asked Elk.

'At the house in Park Lane. He's got the whole story for us. I've arranged to have a police stenographer at nine o'clock tonight.'

At nine o'clock the bearded man sat in Mr Harlow's library; and began in hesitant tones to tell his amazing story.

26

'MY NAME is Stratford Selwyn Mortimer Harlow and as a child I lived as you know with my aunt, Miss Mercy Harlow, a very rich and eccentric lady, who assumed full charge of me and quarrelled with my other aunts over the question of my care.

'I do not remember very distinctly the early days of my life. I have an idea, which Marling confirms, that I was a backward child – backward mentally, that is to say – and that my condition caused the greatest anxiety to Miss Mercy, who lived in terror lest I became feeble-minded and she was in some way held responsible by her sisters. This fear became an obsession with her, and I was kept out of the way whenever visitors called at the house, and practically saw nobody but Miss Mercy, her maid Mrs Edwins, and her maid's son Lemuel, who on two occasions was, I believe, substituted for me – he being a very healthy child.

'I know nothing about the circumstances of his birth, but it is a fact that he was never called by the name of Edwins, except by Miss Mercy, and she continued to call him this even after the time came for him to go to school and the production of his birth certificate made it necessary that he should bear the name of his father, Marling.

'He was my only playmate; and I think that he was genuinely fond of me and that he pitied what he believed to be my weakness of intellect. Mrs Edwins' ambition for her son was unbounded; she strived and scraped to send him to a public school, and when he got a little older (as he told me himself) she prevailed upon Miss Mercy to give her the money to send him to the university.

'Let me say here that I owe most of my information on the subject to Marling himself – it seems strange to call him by a name which I have borne so long! At that time my mind was undoubtedly clouded. He has described me as a morose, timid boy, who spent day after day in a brooding silence, and I should say that that description was an accurate one.

'The fear that her relatives might discover my condition of mind was a daily torment to Miss Mercy. She shut up her house and went to live at a smaller house in the country; and whenever her sisters showed the slightest inclination to visit her, she would move to a distant town. For three years I saw very little of Marling, and then one day Miss Mercy told me that she was engaging a tutor for me. I disliked the idea, but when she said it was Marling I was overjoyed. He came to Bournemouth to see us and I should not have known him, for he had grown a long golden beard, of which he was very proud. We had long talks together and he told me of some of his adventures and of the scrapes he had got into.

'I was the only person in whom he confided, and I know the full story of Mrs Gibbins as she was called. He had met her when she was a pretty housemaid in the service of the senior proctor. The courtship followed a tumultuous course, and then one day there arrived at Oxford the girl's mother, who threatened that unless Marling married her daughter, she would inform the senior proctor. This threat, if it were carried out meant ruin to him, the end of Miss Mercy's patronage, the destruction of all his mother's hopes; and it was not surprising that he took the easiest course. They were married secretly at Cheltenham and lived together in a little village just outside the city of Oxford.

'Of course the marriage was disastrous for Marling. He did not love the girl; she hated him with all the malignity that a common and ignorant person can have for one whose education emphasised her own uncouthness. The upshot of it was that he left her. Three years later he learnt from her mother that she was dead. In point of fact that was not true. She had contracted a bigamous marriage with a man named Smith, who was eventually killed in the war. You have told me, Mr Carlton, that you found no marriage certificate in her handbag.

'By this time, owing to circumstances which I will explain, Marling had the handling of great wealth. He was oddly generous, but the pound a week which he allowed his wife's mother was, I suspect, in the nature of a thanksgiving for freedom. The money came regularly to her every quarter and while she suspected who the sender was, she had no proof and was content to go on enjoying her allowance. Later this was improperly diverted to her daughter, who, on the death of her mother, assumed her maiden name.

'Marling came to be my tutor, and I honestly think that under his care – I would almost say affectionate guidance – I improved in health, though I was far from well, when Miss Mercy had her seizure. In my crazy despair I remember I accused Marling of killing her, for I saw him pour the contents of a green bottle into a glass and force it between Miss Mercy's pale lips. I am convinced that I did him a grave injustice, though he never ceased to remind me of that green bottle. I think it was part of his treatment to keep my illusion before my eyes until I recognised my error.

'On the death of Miss Mercy I was so ill that I had to be locked in my room, and it was then, I think, that Mrs Edwins proposed the plan which was afterwards adopted, namely, the substitution of Marling for myself. You will be surprised and incredulous when I tell you that Marling never forgave the woman for inducing him to take that step. He told me once that she had put him into greater bondage than that in which I was held. From his point of view I think he was sincere. I was hurried away to a cottage in Berkshire; and I knew nothing of the substitution until months afterwards, when I was brought to Park Lane. It was then that he told me my name was Marling and that his was Harlow. He used to repeat this almost like a lesson, until I became used to the change.

'I don't think I cared very much; I had a growing interest in books and he was tireless in his efforts to interest me. He claimed, with truth, that whatever imprisonment I suffered, he saved me from imbecility. The quiet of the life, the care-free nature of it, the comfort and mental satisfaction which it gave me, was the finest treatment I could have possibly had. He made me acquainted with the pathological side of my case, read me books that explained just why I was living the very best possible life – again I say, he was sincere.

'Gradually the cloud seemed to dissipate from my mind. I could think logically and in sequence; I could understand what I was reading. More and more the extent of the wrong he had done me became apparent. He never disguised the fact, if the truth be told. Indeed, he disguised nothing! He took me completely into his confidence. I knew every coup he engineered in every detail.

'One night he returned to the house terribly agitated, and told me that he had heard the voice of his wife! He had been to the flat of a man called Ingle; and whilst he was there a charwoman had come in and he had recognised her voice.

'He was engaged at that time with Ingle in manoeuvring an amazing swindle. It was none other than the impersonation of the Foreign Minister by Ingle, who was a brilliant actor. The plot was to get the Minister to Park Lane, where he would be drugged and his place taken by Ingle, who, to make himself perfect in the part, had spent a week examining films of Sir Joseph Layton. In this way he had familiarised himself with Sir Joseph's mannerisms; and he had paid one stealthy visit to a public meeting which Sir Joseph had addressed, in order to study his voice. The plan worked. Sir Joseph went into a room with Marling, drank a glass of wine and was immediately knocked out – I think that is the expression. Ingle waited behind the door all ready made up; and Marling told me he bore a striking resemblance to the Minister. He went out from the house, drove to the House of Commons and delivered a war speech which brought the markets tumbling down.

'But before this happened there was a tragedy at 704, Park Lane. Apparently, when Marling approached Ingle the actor-convict had been in some doubt as to whether he should go to meet him. Ingle at first suspected a trap and wrote a letter declining to meet. Afterwards he changed his mind, but left the letter on his writing desk and the charwoman, Mrs Gibbins, seeing the envelope was marked "Urgent, By Hand," came to the conclusion that her master had gone out and forgotten the letter; and with a desire to oblige, she herself brought it to Park Lane. Marling opened the door to her and had the shock of his life, for immediately he recognised her. He invited her into the library and there she slipped on the parquet floor and fell, cutting her head against the corner of the desk. They made every effort to restore her: that I can vouch for. They even brought me down to help, but she was dead, and there arose the question of disposing of the body.

'Marling never ceased to blame himself that he did not call in the police immediately and tell them the truth, but he was afraid to have his name mentioned in connection with a man who had recently been discharged from prison; and in the end he and Mrs Edwins took the body to Hyde Park and dropped it in the water. You tell me there were signs of a struggle, but that is not so. The footprints were Mrs Edwins's and not the dead woman's.

'Marling never saw the letter which the woman brought, it must have fallen from her pocket when they were carrying her down the slope towards the canal. He told me all about it afterwards; and I know he spoke the truth.'

(Here Mr Harlow's narrative was interrupted for two hours as he showed some signs of fatigue. It was resumed at his own request just before midnight.)

'Marling regarded his crimes as jokes, and always referred to them as such. It is, I believe, a common expression amongst the criminal classes and one which took his fancy. The great "joke" about Sir Joseph was the plan to restore him to his friends. I think it was partly Ingle's idea, and was as follows. Two nigger minstrel suits were procured, exactly alike, and it was arranged that Ingle, at a certain hour, should get himself locked up and conveyed to what Marling invariably called "the lifeboat"—'

'Lifeboat?' interrupted Jim quickly. 'Why did he call it that?'

'I will tell you,' resumed Mr Harlow. 'You will remember that he presented a police station which he had built only about fifty yards from this house; he made this presentation with only one idea in his mind: if he were arrested it was to that police station that he would be taken!

'Sir Joseph lay under the influence of drugs in the room off the underground garage until the moment arrived, when he was stripped, his upper lip shaved and his face covered with the black make-up of a minstrel. He was then taken through the little door, which you say you have seen, along a bricked passage to one of the stairways beneath the cells, and the substitution was an easy matter. Every bed in every cell lifts up, if you know the secret, like the lid of a box; beneath each bed is a flight of steps leading to the passage and to the garage—'

Jim ran into Evory Street station.

'I want to see Harlow quick!' he said breathlessly.

'He's all right; he was asleep the last time I saw him,' said the inspector on duty.

'Let me see him,' said Jim impatiently; and followed the jailer down the corridor till they stopped outside Cell No 9.

The jailor squinted through the peep-hole. Suddenly he uttered an exclamation and turned the lock. The cell was empty!

When they visited the garage, the dark blue car was gone; and though this was found later abandoned on the Harwich road, the Splendid Harlow had vanished as though the earth had opened; nor was he ever seen again, though sometimes there came news from the continent of gigantic operations engineered through Spanish banks by an unknown plutocrat.

The Splendid Harlow had cached most of his money in Spain, but though Jim visited that country, he pursued no inquiries.

People on their honeymoon have very little time for criminal investigation.

'If I had only known about that infernal police station!' he said once, as they were loafing through the Puerta del Sol.

Aileen changed the subject at the earliest possible moment. For she had known about the plank beds which were doors to freedom.

It was too good a joke for Harlow to keep to himself. And in telling her he ran very little risk. He was an excellent judge of human nature.